Feel-Good Stories

Feel-Good Stories

Sarah Swatridge

Sarah Swatridge

© Copyright 2024
Sarah Swatridge
The right of Sarah Swatridge to be identified as author of this work has been asserted by her in accordance with the Copyright, Designs and Patents Act 1988

All rights reserved

No parts of this publication may be reproduced, stored in a retrieval system, or transmitted in any form or by any means, electronic, mechanical, photocopying, recording or otherwise without prior permission of the copyright owner.

British Library Cataloguing in Publication Data
A Record of this Publication is available from the British Library

ISBN 978-1-914199-62-2

This edition published 2024 by Bridge House Publishing
Manchester, England

Contents

Introduction

Feel Good Stories is a collection of short tales chosen to make you laugh, cry and generally feel all the better for having read them. There's something for everyone, modern, historical, coping with what life throws at you, romance, loss and a good dose of humour.

The Feast

Set in Wales around 1920

Bethan walked slowly down the back staircase, deep in thought. On the bottom step, she paused, and took a deep breath. Her first job was to see Mr Thomas, the Head Butler. He would need to be told of Lady Anwen's decision.

She jumped as Mr Thomas emerged from the staff dining hall and almost collided with her.

"Well?" he asked.

"I got it!" she blurted out and gave him a big grin. Then, composing herself, she added, more formally, "Lady Anwen has kindly offered me the role of housekeeper, so I can follow in Granny's footsteps after all."

"Congratulations Bethan, I had every confidence in you. I suppose now we'll all have to address you as Mrs Morgan?"

"Mrs?"

"Yes, you're married to the job, so don't forget that."

Despite his sober warning, he gently pushed open the double doors to the dining hall to reveal practically all the members of the household, the staff, that is. It seemed they were eagerly awaiting her news. This motley group of people had become family to her, and it gave her a warm glow to know they were behind her, with the exception perhaps of Gwyneth.

A cheer went up and several of the maids came forward to give her a hug.

"I knew you could do it," Nerys told her. "I suppose you'll be moving down here now?"

"Dyfan! George! Come and help Mrs Morgan move her belongings," ordered Mr Thomas.

"Oh, I'm not ready yet. You'll need to give me a few minutes to pack up." She told the butler. Leaning closer, she whispered, "Who is George?"

"The new footman, a wounded soldier, but eager to help. He arrived earlier."

That evening Mrs Jones, the cook, put on a more lavish meal than usual for the staff and the Master, being the generous man he was, told Mr Thomas that each member of staff could enjoy a glass of wine with their meal, so long as it didn't affect their ability to work."

"One glass each mind," Mr Thomas warned as Dyfan carried bottles up from the cellar.

It didn't take long for Bethan to pack up her belongings and to move from the attic room she shared with Nerys, down to the housekeeper's lounge on the ground floor.

"Settled in?" Mr Thomas asked from the open doorway.

"Oh Mr Thomas, I don't think I'll ever get used to this," Bethan admitted. She waved her arms about the room. "I've never had my own room."

Mr Thomas coughed. "May I come in?" he asked formally.

"Of course," Bethan told him. She'd known Mr Thomas all her life. His family had grown up on the estate just as she had done. In fact, most of the forty staff members were related in some way or another.

Mr Thomas quietly closed the door and stepped into the housekeeper's lounge. At least that was what it was referred to, but in actual fact, it was a large room divided into three areas. There was a pair of comfortable chairs around the fireplace where Bethan could read of an evening.

In the corner, by the window, was a bureau for her to keep her accounts in order. Opposite that was another window and to one side was a small, circular table set with two chairs. This would be where the housekeeper could take tea, or interview staff.

On the far wall there was the most enormous dresser. It went from floor to ceiling and stretched along the entire wall. One section housed clean linen needed throughout the house, another stocked the very best of the china only used on high days and holidays, and only by the family. The third section contained a myriad of household items such as the silver punchbowl, Lady Anwen's personal supply of Lavender salts which eased her aches and pains and various cleaning materials.

"If I may be so bold," Mr Thomas began. He stood with his hands behind his back as if he were addressing the Master himself. "The role of housekeeper is a lonely one. You need to distance yourself from the rest of the staff, while still being approachable, should there be a problem. You most certainly cannot have favourites. At all times you need to be on your best behaviour in order to set a good example to the rest of us."

"I do understand," Bethan said. "Granny Morgan prepared me well. It's just…"

Mr Thomas stepped forward. "May I?" he gestured to the fireside chairs.

"Please do,"

Seated together, he continued. "We were all taken by surprise by your grandmother's sudden demise. I know it was always her intention you should follow in her footsteps, and she's trained you well. But, with respect, you are young and will have to earn your respect. It is not going to be easy, but you can count on my support."

"Thank you," Bethan smiled. "I shan't let you down. I'll make sure Granny would be proud of me."

Bethan had already given her new role a great deal of thought. After all she'd been dreaming about being the housekeeper for many years, although hadn't expected it to become reality so soon.

She knew her first, and most important job, was to earn the respect of the staff by working hard and showing that she was perfectly capable of mucking in when it was all hands-on deck, which seemed to happen more often these days.

Once she felt she'd established herself, she then wanted to introduce a few new things. There was little turnover of staff because most jobs were handed down from father to son or mother to daughter. Bethan's own mother had died in childbirth, so she'd been brought up by her grandmother and an aunt.

This aunt now lived with her husband in a nearby village. She was a founder member of the local Women's Institute. Bethan had been impressed by the range of talks that were now on offer to women. But more than that, the WI arranged practical training sessions and Bethan wanted to encourage her maids to join so they could learn flower arranging, cake decorating and other useful skills.

However, that evening when she joined the rest of the staff for the evening meal, she met her first challenge. It was one she'd not anticipated.

"It's the best day of the year," Nerys was explaining to George, the new footman. "We move the tables out into the courtyard and dance until dawn."

Colour rose in Bethan's cheeks; she managed to mask it from all but the watchful Mr Thomas. Nothing ever went unnoticed as far as he was concerned.

Nerys continued to describe the Twelfth Night meal and all the preparation that went into it. She rose and skipped along the flagstones until she caught Bethan's disapproving eye and sat down again. "The Master and the rest of the family come down here, imagine, to the kitchens! He has the first dance with the housekeeper, and then they bid us goodnight and thankfully, turn a blind eye in the morning if we're all a bit sleepy."

Later that evening when all was quiet, Bethan went to call on Mr Thomas before he prepared for bed.

"But I can't dance!" she told him. "I'm sure Granny Morgan would have taught me but..."

"Leave it with me," Mr Thomas told her.

The following days were very busy as they prepared the house for the Christmas festivities. Thankfully everyone was in good spirits, only the Master was out of sorts as he'd gone down with a cold in the head.

Mrs Jones was appreciative of Bethan's help in the kitchen as the family announced, somewhat late, that they had guests coming for Christmas.

Each evening Bethan sat alone by the fire at the end of the day and said her prayers. She felt it too extravagant to light the fire in her bedroom.

"Amen," she said and looked up. She was sure she'd heard a knock. "Who is it?"

"George Watkins," came the reply. "Mr Thomas has sent me."

"How can I help?" Bethan told him as she pulled her shawl around her.

George was from over the Welsh border but despite his English accent he was proving a valuable member of the household. He had a pleasant disposition and willingly offered his help. He certainly hadn't gone unnoticed by the maids. He carried himself well and was light on his feet, just occasionally she'd noticed a slight limp.

In truth she probably would never have been aware of it, but she'd caught Gwyneth mimicking him. Bethan took her aside and reprimanded her.

"I understand you need dance lessons," he said quietly. "Don't be alarmed. Mr Thomas has briefed me well. I shall be discreet. No one need ever know. He'll be joining us in a moment."

"In that case, Mr Watkins, you'd better come in and shut the door."

A few minutes later Mr Thomas arrived and with George's help they assembled a gramophone on the table. Mr Thomas made himself comfortable with the newspaper while George instructed Bethan. Fortunately, the household was steeped in tradition, so everyone knew exactly which dance she needed to know.

This happened each evening for the next week. Bethan was not a natural dancer but George was reassuring.

"The man always leads, so you have nothing to worry about, just follow what he does."

At first Bethan kept stepping on George's toes, or moving left instead of right. He was patient and charming. It surprised Bethan how much she looked forward to her nightly dances. It was a wonderful feeling being held in his arms.

"How did you learn to dance so well?" she asked.

"After the war I worked for a large family with a predominance of girls. There were seven daughters and numerous maiden aunts. Male dancing partners were in short supply and it became part of the footman's duties to step in, so to speak, in order that none of the ladies felt left out."

"Well, we are very fortunate to have you and I am so grateful," Bethan told him.

"You seem to have mastered it now," Mr Thomas remarked as he carefully folded his newspaper. "One further practise on the eve of the feast should suffice."

"But..." Bethan began, she was reluctant to let go of George's hand and was pleased to see he continued to hold her at the waist, "perhaps just a little longer?"

"It's our Twelfth Night feast, not the Grand Ball!" Mr Thomas said and ushered George away.

Christmas was a jolly occasion despite the additional workload due to elaborate meals, extra guests, and gowns to be repaired. Bethan kept her maids fully occupied and made sure she lowered her eyes if George came into the room. She missed his easy company and tender encouragement.

On the eve of the feast, Mr Thomas accompanied George to the housekeeper's lounge and set up the gramophone. Bethan had been looking forward to the evening very much.

"There's been a change of plan," Mr Thomas announced. "The Master has taken to his bed. He's not at all well. Lady Anwen has arranged for his younger brother to step in and take the first dance. He is aware of his duties, so this shouldn't be an issue. In fact, it'll be more like dancing with George, than the Master, and you seem to be enjoying that."

Bethan glanced up and met George's sorrowful eyes. "Maybe I can be permitted to have a dance with you once the family have gone back upstairs?"

She looked in Mr Thomas' direction. "The Head Butler and Housekeeper generally retire early, so that everyone can relax and enjoy themselves without feeling inhibited," Bethan explained.

"Maybe on this occasion," Mr Thomas said, "we could stay for a dance, or two, but no more."

Lady Anwen had kindly given Bethan her oldest gown. It had been adjusted so many times the material was wearing thin. Bethan had asked Gwyneth to repair it.

Nerys kindly offered to be Bethan's lady's maid.

"Thank you but I must speak to Gwyneth first," Bethan said. "Gwyneth, may I have a word?" The girl looked sour. "You've done a marvellous job with Lady Anwen's gown. Is needlework something you enjoy?"

"I do. It beats cleaning any day."

"I can't guarantee you won't be needed to clean, but you'll be my first choice if there's sewing or mending to be done." For the first time Gwyneth's face broke into a smile, and she gave a little curtsey.

Nerys expertly arranged Bethan's hair. "You look like a real lady," she said.

Mrs Jones excelled herself and put on a superb supper for them all on the evening of Twelfth Night. Once the feast was over, the menfolk carried the long wooden benches into the courtyard and the flagstone floor was swept as the musicians set up by the fireplace. There would be no need for a fire this evening as everyone would be warmed by the ale and the dancing.

Bethan had picked at her meal, anxious that she would make a fool of herself. It would undo the work she'd done to present herself as the wise and capable housekeeper.

The musical introduction began. The Master's younger brother stepped forward and gave her a bow. Taking her hand, he led her to the middle of the dance floor. Bethan had never seen the gentleman up close. Although he resembled the Master, he could have been his son, rather than his brother. The maids would be so envious but her grandmother would have loved it!

Bethan took a deep breath and concentrated on the task in hand. George had taught her well, but it was like her first lesson. She was rigid with fear and didn't relax until the ordeal was over. The family ascended the stairs and the real fun began.

Dyfan stood on the bottom step, so he could be seen, and became the caller for the evening. It took the pressure off, and meant anyone could join in because Dyfan told them what they needed to do.

George appeared at her side. "Well done," he whispered. Aloud he said, "Mrs Morgan, may I have the honour of this dance?"

"Thank you, Mr Watkins, it would be a pleasure."

For the first time George and Bethan were able to talk without being overheard. Others promenaded around them.

Even Mr Thomas had scooped Nerys up in his arms and was leading her around the dance floor.

"I was worried the Master would want to stay and dance more, or worse still, take you away with him."

"I very much doubt that," Bethan laughed. "I was so nervous; he must have felt he was dancing with a washboard!"

"You seem relaxed now,"

"I am. Thank you so much for your help. I'm in your debt," she told him.

"Maybe you can help me," George said. "In my previous household, they held regularly monthly dances, not just for them upstairs, but for servants too, obviously in separate venues. Everyone agreed it made the servants feel like a big family and we worked together better."

"I see," Bethan said with a big smile.

"I thought you might, but what about Mr Thomas? We'd need his approval."

Together they glanced over toward the Head Butler who was still dancing. This time with Gwyneth.

"I think, perhaps," Bethan said, "that might not be as difficult as we thought. Leave it with me."

Bethan allowed herself two further dances and then slipped out of the room to allow the maids their freedom from her watchful eyes. Reluctant as she was to leave the dancing, she was looking forward to mulling over George's suggestion. This was exactly the sort of thing she'd been hoping to introduce. She knew from experience how hard they all worked. An evening such as tonight would lift the spirits. A happy household would be more efficient to run which would, in turn, make her life easier… and yes, she'd have the perfect excuse to dance with George once more.

Originally published in *My Weekly* in January 2021.

Blessings and Birds

Taking part in the Big Garden Birdwatch each year had become a tradition in the Townsend household.

Debbie settled herself on the sofa in front of the patio doors. The smell of freshly ground coffee always made her feel good, and this morning she'd treated herself to croissants, warm from the oven.

She plumped up the cushions, lay the rug over the arm of the chair, it was January after all, and chose some classical music to play quietly in the background. The only thing missing… was her beloved Jeff.

Last week, she'd almost decided not to bother with the birdwatching weekend; it wouldn't be the same without him. Then her friends, Karen and Liz, fellow widows, said they were participating – so they agreed a time and armed with bird-books, settled down for an hour in front of the birdfeeder, each in their own homes.

It wasn't long before Karen texted to say she'd already seen eight gold-finches! She did have a large garden with lots of mature trees.

Then Liz messaged her – two collared doves. Debbie had dutifully filled up her birdfeeders with a variety of nuts and seeds. She'd washed out the birdbath too, what more could her feathered friends want on this crisp and bright January morning?

Still nothing. She bit into her croissant and savoured the flaky pastry and soft centre; her homemade marmalade complimented it perfectly, as did the vanilla flavoured coffee.

Karen added two blackbirds, one magpie and one robin to her list of sightings. Nothing more from Liz. Debbie was just about to get up and check next door's cat wasn't sitting on the fence, looking menacing, when she was rewarded by a bluetit pecking away at the suet balls.

After that, her robin appeared, followed by a pair of blackbirds, a couple of pigeons and a Dunnock.

By the end of the hour, she had a respectable list, unless you compared it with Karen's or Liz's. No worries, the garden watch was over three days, she'd repeat the exercise on Saturday and Sunday and choose the best.

As Debbie began to clear up, she reached out for the bird-books and a handful of papers fell out of Jeff's tatty old book. One was a Christmas card with a robin on a feeder. She opened the card and was surprised to see it was from her to Jeff.

"I must have given it to him over forty years ago, and he kept it all that time," she told Liz later when they met up for a walk.

"How romantic," Liz teased.

"He probably only kept it for the robin," Debbie joked, but inside she was touched by the thought that the card had meant so much to him. They'd had their first date in January, perhaps he'd been prompted by the card? It had been her not-so-subtle way of showing she liked him.

"Did you find anything else?" Liz asked.

"There was a beautiful photograph of a pigeon,"

"A pigeon!" Liz chuckled. "You sound like my granddaughter; she loves to feed them." Liz used to see Poppy most days, but now she was at school, she rarely saw her.

"When you look closely, they do have beautiful colours," continued Debbie in defence of the pigeon, but Liz had lost interest.

"Any plans for later on?" Liz asked.

"I'm tempted to go to the garden centre and buy another feeding station," Debbie said. "Not that I'm competing with Karen."

On Saturday morning, Debbie repeated her ritual, and sat down by the window, giving her a good view of the garden especially the bird feeder.

This time she saw more bluetits and a coaltit as well as a "USB".

"What's that?" Liz asked when they met for their daily walk.

"An Unidentified Small Bird," Debbie explained. "I meant to look it up. I'll do it when I get home," she said as her phone pinged.

She read her message; her son and daughter-in-law wanted to go to the cinema and wondered if she could babysit.

"No problem," Debbie texted her son, "but it would suit me if Ben had a sleepover. It would also mean you get a lie-in on a Sunday morning."

"Don't you want one?" her son asked, calling for a chat.

"I never have a lie-in," Debbie said. "Besides, I want to get up and watch the birds."

"You're lucky," Liz said, "I hardly get to see Poppy these days."

As soon as Debbie got home, she reached for the bird books. His and Hers. Jeff's was ancient and full of detailed sketches and pages of facts, whereas hers was bought more recently, at a National Trust shop. The digital photography was excellent but there were just a few bullet points on each bird. The two books complimented each other, just as she and Jeff had done.

Not long afterwards, Ben arrived with his parents. Her grandson was four and very chatty. He was a frequent visitor and they had their own little routine. They played with the box of toys, then had tea, bath and a story, then sleep.

On Sunday morning, Ben clambered on to the sofa, sitting where Jeff had always sat.

Debbie had primed him. He had his own bird book, and

a pair of binoculars as well as a clip-board so he could record his own sightings.

"That's a robin," she explained and Ben nodded knowledgably. "Oh, and that big black and white one's a magpie."

"What's that. Grandma?" he asked pointing excitedly to the pigeon pecking away on the ground underneath the birdfeeder.

"That's a pigeon." She showed him the picture in the book. "We're doing well this morning." She sipped her coffee, breathing in the calming aroma of vanilla.

"Look!" shouted Ben.

"That's a blackbird," Debbie said, noting it down.

"No, no, that one." Ben stood up on the sofa and pointed. "It's not black it's brown."

"A female blackbird is brown," Debbie explained patiently to which Ben looked at his grandmother in sheer disbelief. "It's true," she said. His face was a picture. His eyes were wide, his natural smile grew into a big grin before he burst into giggles.

It was infectious and before long, Debbie too was laughing with him.

"Oh quick, look a wren, that tiny one in the flower pot." They watched the wren for a little while before Ben asked what was eating the berries.

"My goodness, that's a fieldfare, I've only ever seen one of those… in Karen's Garden." It was only then she realised her phone had been silent, nothing from Karen and nothing from Liz. Perhaps they'd opted for a lie-in?

When Ben's parents came to fetch him, he proudly told them of all the birds they'd seen. He tried to whistle like the kite but then recalled the brown blackbird and once again couldn't control his giggles.

"We'll have to do it again next year," Debbie told him as she gave him a hug goodbye.

"Can't we do it again next week?" he asked, giving her a look that so reminded her of Jeff. "I want to see the parrow."

"You saw a parrot?" asked his mum in surprise. "Are you sure?"

"No." He laughed again. "A parrow." He reached for his picture book and pointed a chubby little finger at one of the pictures.

"I was telling him, when I was young, we used to see loads of sparrows in the hedgerows, but nowadays, I hardly see any, and then, bless my soul, but we see one on the hedge at the back." Debbie smiled.

After they'd gone, Debbie cleared the coffee table, picking up the bird books and her three lists, one from Friday, one from Saturday and the ones she and Ben had made earlier that day.

She slipped Ben's into Jeff's reference book, along with his memorabilia. As she did so, she came across their record sheets from previous years.

Debbie settled back down on the settee and flicked through them, carefully putting them in date order. They'd lived in the same house for years. However, when they'd moved in, the house was new, and the garden sparse. Now it was full of mature trees and shrubs. The hedgerows hid the fence panels and were laden with berries, chosen to attract a wide range of wildlife. They had several bird boxes as well as the birdbath and feeders. No wonder her list grew longer each year.

Debbie's hand shook as she picked up one piece of yellowing paper, so old the lines were feint.

As with so many things in their lives, tasks were divided

between them, Jeff washed up, and she dried; She did the hoovering, he mowed the lawn. When it came to birdwatching, he usually held the binoculars and she acted as scribe, but this old list was in Jeff's distinctive handwriting.

Debbie's eyes filled with tears and for a moment or two, she sat quietly and let herself wallow in his memory. He'd always been a good husband and father to their son. Of course, they'd had their moments, but theirs had been a long and happy marriage spanning over forty years.

Eventually, she wiped her eyes, took a deep breath and looked again at the sheet in front of her. His writing had never been easy to read. Seeing the date, 1986, she realised why they'd swapped tasks; she'd been heavily pregnant with their son. Jeff had insisted she lay back on the sofa, put her feet up, and stare out of the window, with or without the binoculars.

The memories came flooding back: happy times. He'd be so pleased by Ben's interest this morning and thrilled that he wanted to do it again so soon.

That evening, Debbie entered her data onto the computer using their online form and pressed send. She then emailed both Liz and Karen with her results, even though she was meeting them the following day.

"A fieldfare?" Karen gasped as she went through Debbie's list on her phone. "I don't seem to get them anymore, but then we have chopped back a lot of hedges at the front to let in more light."

"So, what did you see yesterday?" Debbie asked the two of them. Karen instantly reeled off an impressive list, even if it didn't include a fieldfare. "And you?" she asked Liz.

"I only saw a robin on Saturday," she admitted, "so I didn't even bother on Sunday."

“Oh, don’t say that!” Debbie said quickly. “I used to dismiss sparrows as boring, but now they’re so rare, rather like hedgehogs. You never see them nowadays. We’ve got to appreciate what we *have* got.”

“But just one robin when I’d spent a small fortune on bird food and given up a whole hour just to sit. It was as bad as watching grass grow. I shan’t be doing that again.”

Karen spotted a neighbour of hers and went to show them the video clip on her phone of the charm of goldfinches feeding in her garden.

“So, what’s really up?” Debbie asked as she leant forward so no one would hear. “It’s not like you to be so miserable.”

“My daughter’s not pregnant at all; she’s just put on weight. In fact, she wants me to babysit Poppy regularly on a Tuesday night, so she can go to her slimming class.”

“Oh well, you’ll love that,” Debbie reminded her.

“I know, but for years I’ve been hoping Poppy could have a brother or sister and then I’d convinced myself she was going to tell me the good news. I felt so disappointed.”

“Only the other day, you said you didn’t see enough of Poppy; you should be delighted.”

“I am,” Liz smiled and finished her coffee. “You’re right, I should appreciate what I do have.”

Originally published in *My Weekly* in January 2022.

Hey Mr Postman!

Simon, the postman, looked again at the postcard. It definitely said "49 Franklin Avenue" and yet there only seemed to be thirty well-established homes.

He was fairly new to the area, having moved on his thirtieth birthday! Perhaps there was a Franklin Road, Street or Crescent? He checked his phone. The signal wasn't great but eventually he found there were no other similar road names.

Of course, that didn't account for any new-builds. It seemed to take an age before new postcodes were updated.

He studied the postcard. The picture was of a bunch of roses. The warmth of the red made him smile. They cheered him on a bitterly cold February morning. It was almost Valentine's Day; this card could be really important…

It was addressed to Lizzie Halladay, so he looked up that name, but the search wasn't helpful. Time was getting on and he needed to finish his round. He slipped the postcard in his pocket and continued on his way.

He returned to the depot and spoke to his supervisor. Together they examined the postcard but even the postmark wasn't clear. They had no clue as to who had sent it. It wasn't even signed, and the message seemed rather cryptic.

"So, what do we do now?" Simon asked.

"There's nothing more we can do." His boss shook his head. "The policy is to place it in the 'undelivered'" tray for one month, after which it's shredded and the paper recycled."

Simon wasn't happy with that. "I don't like to stand in the way of true love," he said. "Can I try and track her down?"

"Not officially," his supervisor said, then added, "It'll have to be in your own time. "And don't do anything to give the post office a bad name! And remember, we haven't had this conversation?"

Once Simon had finished his shift, he returned home to his empty flat and fixed himself a bite to eat. There was no "significant other" in his life, and having only recently moved to the area, he hadn't yet made friends.

His time was his own, and he loved a challenge. It didn't take long to design a poster: "Are you Lizzie Halladay? *Urgent* Letter waiting for you at the post office. Bring ID."

Just as he was about to press "print", his supervisor's words came back to him, "Don't do anything to give the post office a bad name." This wasn't part of their policy; but he could still ask around.

Perhaps it wasn't number forty-nine at all? But number four or number nine? It was a bit of a longshot, but worth a try. He grabbed his coat and went back in the direction of Franklin Avenue.

"Sorry to bother you," he said as a heavily pregnant woman at number 4 answered the door. "You wouldn't be Lizzie Halladay, would you?"

"Not me," she said. "Why do you ask?"

Simon explained and the woman told him it wouldn't be number nine as it was empty; the elderly occupier having died some months ago.

"No worries, just worth a try," he said cheerfully. "Here's my number if you think of anything."

"Good luck, hope you find her."

Simon began to concentrate more on the message. Was it in code? He woke at 3 a.m. in a cold sweat. He was wide awake with a feeling he had the answer on the tip of his tongue.

He lay in bed trying to recall the cryptic clue from the card. *If you're not a Gillian Flynn female, then Lindisfarne. X.*

The more he thought, the more complicated it sounded. He dozed a while but woke, as usual, at six and got up to make tea and toast. It being his day off, he took them back to bed, listening to the radio.

Chrissie Cala was the DJ; she was inviting people to share their Valentine's stories to get people in the mood for this romantic of all days.

Simon reached for his phone and briefly told the receptionist his dilemma.

"Now here we have a chance to unite two people," Chrissie Cala was saying, "I'll let a local Postie explain…"

Simon was careful not to give away any personal data.

"I've got a postcard to deliver to a lady but her address doesn't exist," he began and gave a concise list of all the things he'd tried so far. "The card says 'If you're not a Gillian Flynn female, then Lindisfarne.' And it's signed with a kiss."

"So, if this means something to you, or anyone can shed any light, now's your chance to get in touch." Chrissie Cala played a popular song and chatted to Simon while his tea went cold. "And how many Valentines have you sent?"

"Me? None," Simon felt he had to explain. "I've only just moved here and I don't know anyone yet."

Back on air, Chrissie told her audience what a great response they'd had already, calls, emails, texts.

"Margaret on London Road says – Gillian Flynn wrote Gone Girl, so does that mean, if you're not a gone girl… if you've not gone away? Would that make sense?"

"Maybe it would, but I still don't have the correct address for her," Simon explained. "All I know is that 49 Franklin Avenue isn't right."

Chrissie chatted away like an old friend while the adverts played. On air she said, "Perhaps this will help? Liam says at the university there are several halls of residence and one's called Franklin. There are about fifty studio flats – maybe she's there?"

"That's definitely worth a try, especially if she's is studying Literature and has read *Gone Girl*?"

"Matt has emailed; he reckons it means, if you're not a Gone Girl, that is, moved away, then 'Meet me on the corner' – a Lindisfarne hit, AND there is The Corner Café. The next line of the song is 'when the lights are coming on… The Corner Café opens at 7 a.m., could Lover Boy be sitting there waiting for his girl?' "

The voices faded out and Lindisfarne's hit song played. Simon heard the chorus, "Meet me on the corner when the lights are coming on…"

By now, Simon was back out of bed and dressing. His plan was to head straight down to the Corner Café to make sure everyone knew of this potential rendezvous.

"OK, Simon the postman," the DJ continued, "you must promise you'll call me if you are successful with your match-making. Listen out tomorrow folks for more romantic Valentine stories…"

He found the café, which had opened at seven to serve cooked breakfasts.

Once more, he told his story and left his number… just in case.

"I'm going to see if I can find Flat 49 Franklin Block."

The university campus was close by; a site map showed him where to go. Usually, all mail was left in a pile on the floor at the communal entrance. Someone had begun to sort it into piles – first floor, second floor and so on.

He knocked on the door marked forty-nine, but there was no reply.

"She's given up, moved out," a neighbour told him as he fumbled with his key. By the look of him, the student seemed to be coming home from a night out, his hair dishevelled and his clothes creased.

"Who lived here?" Simon asked, and held his breath.

"Elizabeth. A mature student. She never chatted much. About a fortnight ago, she packed her bags and disappeared. University's not for everyone. There's always a percentage who drop out."

"And you don't know her full name or have a forwarding address?" Simon asked feeling yet again it was one step forward and another back again.

"I didn't really know her, she never fitted in. She seemed quite miserable, if you ask me. The Admin Office would have her details."

It was still early, and the administrative centre didn't open until nine. Simon returned to the Corner Café and ordered a fresh cup of tea and a bacon butty. He read the paper from cover to cover; something he never got to do.

Feeling full, and optimistic, he approached the university Admin Office and repeated the whole story.

"I can't give out any personal information on any of our students," the woman told him.

"I understand." Simon nodded. "But you could call her and give her my number and ask her to call me? It could be important – a life changing moment."

"I shouldn't really," the woman hesitated. "Give me ten minutes and be prepared that she might not want to be contacted." Simon nodded.

He paced up and down, wondering why he'd not just filed the postcard in the undelivered tray and left it at that.

His phone rang. It wasn't Lizzie but Chrissie from the radio station. "Are you able to come in to the studio tomorrow morning for the breakfast show?" she asked.

"Pardon?"

"We've been inundated with calls and messages saying how good it is to hear of someone going the extra mile to do his job. You're a real hero and I'd really like you to be our Valentine's Celebrity Guest."

"Thanks, but I'm on an early shift tomorrow," he said. "But I promise I'll call and leave a message if I do have any joy."

No sooner had that call ended, when his phone rang again; unlike Chrissie's bright and breezy DJ voice, this voice was quiet and hesitant.

"Hello? My name's Elizabeth Halladay, the university said you were trying to get hold of me."

Yet again, Simon went through the story. "I've got the postcard, safe and sound at work, you just need to come in with some ID."

"Thank you, but I know who it's from; he's found me already. My husband and I were going through a difficult patch. I felt he was always putting me down, so, behind his back, I applied to university. My intention was to get a degree and prove to him I'm not stupid. I walked out last October and ever since, he's been trying to find me. He'd finally tracked me down, having left all sorts of weird messages for me – in newspapers, shop windows, graffiti on walls and on hundreds of notice boards up and down the country. I never knew he cared. I missed him, my home, my friends. I'm doing my studies online now. I'm determined to get that degree!"

"Can I share your story with Chrissie Cala from the breakfast show and the thousands of radio listeners?" Simon asked.

"Don't worry. I'll do it. I'll call her now. And thanks, I appreciate you trying to deliver the card. It was over and above your call of duty, and at least I can say he does appreciate me now, so it's a happy ending."

The alarm went off at 6 a.m., Simon got up and began his daily routine showering and dressing in his post office uniform. Having had such an awful night previously, he'd slept soundly and was looking forward to going to work.

He was surprised by the amount of people around at that time in the morning. Somehow, he'd not noticed the Outside Broadcast Unit parked in front of the sorting office.

"What's all this?" Simon asked, looking at the four sacks of cards lined up against the office wall.

"They're for you," his boss smiled. "But I'd rather you did your round first, because it'll take you all day to open them. Pop them in your car later."

"For me?"

"Chrissie Cala happened to mention the local postie hero trying to help someone, even though there was nobody special in his life. It looks like there's a lot of people wanting to meet you."

"And I'm top of the list," a pretty little blonde woman said quietly. She seemed to be saving her loud and confident voice for the programme, but her smile was for him, and him alone.

Previously published in *My Weekly* in February 2023.

Coming of Age

Although Colin was born in 1952 and all his friends were in their late sixties, he was looking forward to the eighteenth anniversary of his birthday on 29th February 2020.

"So, what are *we* going to do to celebrate?" he asked Oliver, his grandson who was due to be eighteen at the beginning of the month.

"Celebrate?"

"Yes – *our* 18th birthdays. What do eighteen-year-olds do nowadays to mark the occasion?"

"Why don't you take your grandfather to the Magpie and Parrot and buy him a pint?" suggested Oliver's mum, Shannon. Colin's eyes lit up.

"You don't know how much I've been looking forward to having a pint with my son and grandson in the bar at The Magpie."

"All that Male Bonding." Shannon laughed and smiled at her father-in-law. "I think you'd better walk."

"Can I come?" asked seventeen-year-old George.

"You'd be very welcome," Grandpa Colin said with a smile, "but PC Nailor will probably be there, and so it'll have to be a cola for you."

"Boring," George said. It had always been hard on him being only nine months younger than his brother. Colin knew that feeling only too well, he'd been barely a year younger than his brother.

"Don't worry," Grandpa Colin said quickly. "I've put you on my car insurance, so I can take you out in the car and we can practice reversing and parking,"

"Thanks Grandpa,"

"Hey, don't look so glum," Colin said. "You know I'm

going to spoil you rotten next year when it's your eighteenth?"

Shannon knew how important this special birthday was to her father-in-law. He'd reminded her often enough, so she made sure she'd had a quiet word with the landlord of The Magpie and Parrot before the end of the month.

"He has mentioned it once or twice," laughed the landlord. "So, believe me I'm going to make sure he's got some sort of ID on him, otherwise I won't serve him."

Colin had a huge smile on his face from the moment he woke on 29th February. He'd waited long enough for this day to arrive and was determined to make the most of it. It was all the more special that he was surrounded by his family, especially with grandson Oliver having just turned eighteen.

Colin had been widowed a few years previously. He'd sold their old home and bought the house next door to Joe and Shannon, his son and daughter-in-law. He reckoned he had the best of both worlds, family close by whilst maintaining his independence.

Shannon invited him over for a birthday breakfast and was in the process of making everyone bacon sandwiches for a treat. A huge helium balloon bounced around on the kitchen table every time someone moved. As usual, Shannon had the radio on in the background as she grilled the bacon and made copious pots of tea.

"Listen!" she shouted and the whole family fell silent.

"I've been told to repeat his name, so Colin Carpenter if you're listening, I know it's a very special day for you, especially as your particular birthday only comes around once every four years, so make sure you spend time today with your family and celebrate big time, after all, you're only eighteen once and you've had to wait longer than most for your first legal pint!" The DJ announced for the whole country to hear.

"Cheers," Colin said raising his mug of tea before continuing to open cards and presents from his family. His eyes rested on Shannon. "Thanks for that. I've never heard my name on the radio before!"

The postman was laden with more cards and parcels for the birthday "boy". Colin loved every minute and was thoroughly enjoying the attention.

After breakfast he headed straight for the one remaining Travel Agents where Christine Nailor worked, wife of the local bobby.

Christine had been in his class at school many years ago. Colin had always had a crush on her but she'd chosen to marry Bob Nailor because he looked handsome in his uniform and was fifteen years her junior. Colin reminded her of this every so often and they all enjoyed a bit of friendly banter.

However, Colin spent the next hour in her shop trying to book an 18 to 30 holiday without success. Having wasted an hour of her time, whilst drinking her coffee, he gallantly offered to buy her a drink if she cared to come along to The Magpie that evening; he even agreed to her bringing along his rival, her toy-boy Bob Nailor.

For years he'd planned this momentous day in his head. Obviously, he would do all the things you can only legally do once you're eighteen but now, at sixty-eight years the reality of getting a tattoo without his parents' consent had lost its appeal. The same went for drinking and smoking.

None the less, it was his birthday and, although it was a cold day, spring and the better weather was surely on its way, so there was much in Colin's life to be optimistic about.

Colin made his way back home to change. He called in at the corner shop for a bag of mint toffees.

“I thought you said you weren’t to have these any-more because of your teeth?” Nancy the shop keeper reminded him.

“I’m not,” Colin said sheepishly, “but it’s my eighteenth birthday and I can’t see the harm in one or two toffees, especially if I promise to suck them.”

“So, it was your name I heard on the radio this morning.” Nancy laughed. “I thought it was.” Nancy added in a few extra sweets before twisting the top of the little white paper bag and handing them over. Colin paid for his sweets and a newspaper and turned to go.

“Hold on a minute!” Nancy called. A moment later she appeared on his side of the counter and much to his surprise gave him a birthday kiss.

“I’m having a pint at The Magpie tonight. I’ll buy you a drink if you’re there.”

“I might just do that.” Nancy laughed. “It’s a long time since I had a drink with an eighteen-year-old!”

And it’s a long time since I had a twinkle in my eye, thought Colin as he almost skipped up the road clutching his toffees and tucking his paper under his arm.

The whole family were celebrating with an early lunch at a local restaurant. Shannon made sure they had a cake with eighteen candles but when the waiters came to sing Happy Birthday they automatically headed toward Oliver and George at the other end of the table.

“This is the Birthday Boy,” Shannon told them and explained the eighteen candles. Colin loved being the centre of attention.

Later, three generations of the Carpenter family strolled along to their local pub. It was chilly and dark, being February, but they were all in good spirits.

“After all you’re not eighteen every day,” Colin kept telling them.

He was delighted to see the pub filled with his old friends and even his elder brother who now lived some distance away.

"Good evening gentlemen," greeted the Landlord. "What can I get you?"

"A pint of the usual," Colin said, beaming from ear to ear.

"I'm afraid the brewery's introduced a new policy," announced the landlord. "I now have to check everyone's ID before I serve them. Do you have any identification on you sir?"

Colin proudly produced his birth certificate, along with his passport, driving licence and a handful of birthday cards all displaying the number 18.

"You're not taking any chances," laughed the landlord as he inspected the documents before slowly pouring a Guinness.

"I'll need to check yours too," the landlord told Joe, Oliver and George, much to everyone's amusement.

"That all seems to be in order," the landlord told them.

True to his word Colin bought drinks for Christine Nailor and Nancy.

"I don't suppose you'd care to call round for a coffee sometime and help me polish off my birthday cake?" he asked Nancy, feeling rather like a foolish teenager.

"Sounds wonderful." Nancy smiled.

"Ah," Colin said. "A pint has never tasted so good." He drained the glass and replaced it on the counter.

"Do you want another one Grandad?" Oliver asked.

"No thanks Oli, for one thing I'll be up in the night, but also I need to keep a clear head because I've promised to take your brother out for a driving lesson tomorrow."

"Excuse me sir," PC Nailor said. He never seemed to be off-duty. "But are you aware you have to be at least twenty-one to supervise someone learning to drive?"

"But I'm…" began Colin.

"Eighteen," the policeman reminded him. "I'm sure that's what I heard you say to the landlord. Good evening."

"But I won't be twenty-one until 2032, George will be twenty-nine years by then. Do you think he'll wait?"

Previously published in *My Weekly* in February 2020.

Choose Your Words Carefully

"You shouldn't do it. It's not honest Joe," snapped Mollie from her chair beside him.

"It's only a bit of harmless fun," said Norah.

"Harmless!" screeched Mollie, waking up at least two of the residents of Dove Farm Nursing Home. "You shouldn't meddle in other people's affairs, especially not affairs of the heart."

Mollie stood up and made her way out of the communal lounge, as quickly as she could, on legs that had seen too many decades.

"What's wrong with Mollie?" asked Heather, the warden.

"Joe's written a song. It's lovely. Read it Joe," urged Norah.

Joe read out his lyrics. When he came to the last line, some of the residents clapped.

Heather looked puzzled. "It's very good Joe. What's made you start writing love songs at your age?"

"That lad you've had on work experience," admitted Joe, "he's had a tiff with his girlfriend, and wants to make up. They sing in a band and he wanted to write a love song for her to show he really does care. I said I'd help, but Madam's got a bee in her bonnet about it!"

"Stop him!" cried Mollie, from the doorway. "Don't let him give that song away," she said to Heather urgently.

"Calm down Mollie, he's only trying to help."

"He'll do more harm than good. It's dishonest, that's what it is."

"She's only jealous," chimed in Norah.

"Not now Norah," soothed Heather as she straightened her crisp, white uniform. "Sometimes I feel more like a referee than a Carer."

"She's bitter and twisted. She should have appreciated Sid when he was alive," continued Norah, unable to let go.

"You leave Sid out of this."

"Ladies please. Why don't I go and make a tray of tea, while you two make up?"

"I'm going to lie down," announced Mollie.

Heather followed her as she went to put the kettle on, but Mollie refused to come out of her room.

"There's no need for all this fuss," began Heather. "And be careful about calling other people dishonest. You're forever telling people you're sixty-nine, but we both know you're nearer seventy-nine."

"Ok. Point taken," agreed Mollie. "But please stop Joe handing over that song."

"I don't know that I can," admitted Heather.

"Well if you can't, maybe I can," said Mollie getting up and making her way along to Joe's room.

"Not you again," said Joe by way of a greeting.

"Just hear me out," asked Mollie. Her voice was tired and pleading.

"You'd better take a seat, if I'm in for a lecture."

"Not a lecture Joe, just a life story. Years ago, when I was a pretty young thing, I was engaged to a nice, solid man, called Sid. Just before we were to get married, I met Phil who worshipped the ground I walked on. He literally swept me off my feet. We knew instantly we were soul mates. I've never met anyone like Phil since." Mollie paused and twisted her wedding ring. "I was just about to tell Sid I couldn't marry him after all, when he, Sid, produced this wonderful poem. I can recite it now." Mollie closed her eyes. "To walk with you…" She wiped away a tear. "It made me think Sid must have hidden depths if he could write poetry like that. So, it was Phil I said goodbye to. I was a coward really. It was easier to stick with good, dependable Sid, than to follow my heart."

Mollie dabbed her eyes with her handkerchief. "Sid hadn't written that poem. There was no passion or romance in him at all. He was a good man, but we were never 'in love'." Mollie gave a deep sigh. "Help the lad if you want to, but don't help him fool his girlfriend. I'd hate her to end up living a life of regret. Words are so important, we must use them well, and you're so talented Joe."

The following afternoon Mollie heard music coming from the lounge. As she feared, Joe was sitting beside the work experience lad who was strumming away on his guitar.

Mollie scowled at Joe, but he beckoned her over. As she got closer, she was able to hear the words. He sang clearly and with passion.

"What do you think?" the young man asked her.

"It's a different song," said Mollie in surprise.

"Joe said he wasn't happy with yesterday's song so he's written this one called Honesty. Do you like it?"

"I love it!" said Mollie with a smile. "Our Joe's very clever, isn't he?"

Previously published in *Ireland's Own St Patrick's Day Edition* in March 2015, writing as Sarah O'Rourke.

Heart to Heart

My heart sank as I stood in the playground with the other mothers, watching Alex's teacher march towards me.

"The head teacher was wondering if you could spare a moment?" she said sternly.

I looked at Alex. He looked down at the trainers he shouldn't have been wearing to school.

Mrs Giles, the head, was a tall, thin woman, with piercing grey eyes. I could easily believe that she didn't miss a thing.

"Do sit down," she said, pointing to a chair. She gestured to another for Alex. We both sat obediently.

"Mrs Marshall," the head teacher began, "I am aware that you have not had an easy time at home lately..."

I didn't know who had told her, but it was true. Scott and I had had another big argument over the amount of time he spent at work, compared with the time he spent at home. He'd stormed out, and had moved into the room above his workshop on the trading estate.

"The staff have been very tolerant with Alex. We have overlooked certain things," she continued, looking at Alex's feet, "but we've reached a point where things cannot be ignored anymore." She paused and sipped from a glass of water.

"What has Alex done?" I asked nervously.

"Last week we had some tables delivered for the library area. Alex's class had a lesson in the library that afternoon, and at the end of the lesson his teacher found that Alex had scratched a picture on one of these brand-new tables."

"Oh Alex," I sighed.

"I think that Alex should be made to put things right," the head teacher said.

I nodded, wondering how much it would cost to repair the damage.

"I thought he could sand down the table and re-polish it. Your husband would know what needs to be done, wouldn't he?" she went on.

"Yes," I answered, "Scott's in the furniture business. He's picking Alex up tomorrow for the weekend."

"Good. In that case he can either bring a sander with him and do the work after school, or they can take the table away."

"I'll pass the message on," I said meekly.

"I think you ought to leave that to Alex," Mrs Giles said, standing up and moving to open the door for us. "And Alex, we don't wear trainers in school, do we?"

"No, Mrs Giles," Alex murmured.

The following day, I went down to the school to fetch Alex so I could take home his dirty PE kit to wash. Scott met us near the school gates. He'd brought his van, and Mrs Giles took us round to the library to pick up the table. Almost immediately, she was called away to the phone.

Scott and I looked at the graffiti. Alex had scratched a heart shape. Above it he'd written quite clearly, *Mum,* and below, *Dad,* with an arrow through the middle of the heart and zigzag lines where it had been broken in two.

"I love Mum, even if you don't," Alex said accusingly.

"Alex," Scott began, "that's not true. I do love your Mum." I overheard him say it, but he didn't look at me. I wondered if he was just saying it to please Alex.

"But you don't show it," Alex said quietly. I thought Scott would tell Alex he was out of order, but instead he looked stunned, lost for words. "You're never at home. You spend all your time at work," Alex continued.

"Alex, enough now," I said as I saw Scott beginning to wince. I knew he deserved it, but I loved him and didn't want to hurt him. Besides, we were in the school library and Mrs Giles could be back at any moment. I didn't want another scene.

"Let's get this table in the van," Scott said, grabbing one end.

The following week was very quiet. Alex was subdued, and I felt guilty about his behaviour every time I went near the school. I felt I wanted to give something back, but I was too embarrassed.

"You're good at sewing," one mum said. "Why don't you make a story sack? They need them in the new library."

It seemed like a good idea. After all, I had studied upholstery at college. That was where I'd met Scott.

She gave me a book and an example of a story sack. It was a brightly coloured bag based on a story. Inside was a cuddly toy resembling the main character, a linked non-fiction book and a game on the same theme.

"The school needs a story sack to go with this book," she said. I looked at it.

Guess How Much I love You was its title. I handed it straight back, but quickly changed my mind.

It wouldn't take me long, and I had some material I could use. It would also set a good example for Alex, and maybe it would even go some way to making things better for him in school.

The following week Alex and Scott returned the table to the school. It looked brand-new again, which was a relief.

"Dad's got something to say," Alex said, when Scott brought him home. My heart missed a beat. Was he going to suggest he came back?

"I've been commissioned to make two chairs. They need upholstering… I'd pay you," he said.

My heart sank. Was that all he wanted to say?

"We always talked about going into business together," I reminded him.

Scott shrugged. "We used to talk about a lot of things,"

he said quietly. "Let me know about the chairs." He turned to go, then glanced back, saying nothing more.

In the morning we had the usual frantic rush to get Alex off to school on time.

"I thought you'd learned your lesson," I snapped as we walked down the road. He didn't seem to know what I was talking about. "The tree," I told him. He looked blank.

"Have you been writing on the tree in the front garden?" Alex stopped walking. Intrigued, he ran back along the road to look at the horse chestnut tree in our front garden. On the bark was a beautifully carved heart that read, *Scott loves Jane.* It hadn't been there before.

"You can't blame me for that," Alex said with a grin. I felt my heart skip a beat and got a familiar fluttery feeling in my stomach. If it hadn't been Alex, then there was only one other possibility…

"Come on, Alex, quickly, we need to get to school," I said.

"What's the rush?" he asked happily, running to try and catch up with my quick march.

"I'm in a rush because as soon as I've dropped you off at school, I need to see your dad about those chairs he mentioned."

But first, I thought to myself, I'll call the hairdresser and see if they can fit me in. I want to make the best impression I can. In some ways, it would be like a first date – only we'd been married for twelve years! Until recently, those had been happy years.

As soon as I got home, I noticed I'd forgotten to return the story sack I'd finished. It would have to wait. I rang the hairdresser and they could fit me in, if I was quick. Then, I rang Scott. My hand was shaking as I pressed the buttons.

"Marshall's Furniture Company," he said in a dull voice.

"Scott? It's me, Jane."

"Oh," he said, sounding pleased to hear from me.

"You said you had some chairs to be upholstered," I began. Then I couldn't help but go on. "You also said we didn't talk any more, and you're right, perhaps we could…"

"How about lunch?" Scott said quickly. It took me by surprise. He always had a working lunch.

"Are you sure you can spare the time?" I said quietly, hoping that it didn't sound sarcastic.

"Well, this is important. Shall I pick you up at one?"

I felt both excited and nervous as I hurried along to the hairdresser. It was busy and I didn't have time to tidy up before Scott arrived. He came half an hour early.

"I couldn't wait," he said. "I wasn't able to concentrate this morning. All I could do was think about you." He stared at me, and although he didn't mention my hair, I could see he liked the way I looked.

"Shall I make us lunch here?" I asked.

"I rather hoped that you might fancy a walk along the river to that café by the lock?" Scott answered.

"We haven't been there for years!" I exclaimed.

"I know," he said quietly.

I looked down at my smart dress and high shoes.

"That tow path used to get quite muddy. I'll quickly put on my jeans and flat shoes."

When I returned, Scott was looking at the story sack I'd made. I'd chosen white material with little red hearts and I'd appliqued on the front, "*Guess How Much I Love You* by Sam McBratney". Scott smiled at me and reached out his hand.

"Come on, let's go for our walk," he said.

It seemed so natural to walk hand in hand with the man I loved, as we made our way along the river. We were quiet at first, although my heart was pounding loudly. When I did speak, I sounded breathless.

"How's business?"

"Busy."

"I'm sorry," both of us said together, and then we laughed.

"I just want to provide a nice home for you and Alex, I want us to be able to go on holiday and not have to worry too much about money," Scott said urgently.

"I know," I told him, reaching out to hug him. "I should have been more understanding, but I hated it when you were spending all your evenings and weekends at work. Alex and I hardly saw you."

"I received a letter the other day, asking me if I'd consider taking on an apprentice. I'd be eligible for a grant, so it wouldn't really cost me much, and it would make a real difference to the business. It would also give this lad a start in life."

"I can help, too," I said, squeezing his arm tightly.

"I know. We used to be quite a good team before Alex was born."

I wanted to ask if we could try again, but the words just wouldn't come out. I was too afraid of rejection. Scott cradled my face in his hands.

"I've missed you so much," he said.

"Come back home to us," I said, and he was already nodding his head. I couldn't help shedding a few tears. He kissed me gently and then, with renewed vigour we walked to the café.

Over lunch we talked excitedly about working together again and then about the holiday we'd have in the summertime.

Scott even suggested that we decorate Alex's bedroom. We hadn't decorated for years and the place could do with some love and attention.

"This is great," I said. "It's just like old times, only better, because I appreciate everything so much more, now."

"Me too," Scott agreed.

Just then I noticed his watch. "Don't you need to rush back to work?" I asked. Scott looked at the time.

"I haven't had a day off since I moved out, so I think we deserve a few hours. How about we have another coffee here, and then a slow walk home and collect Alex together from school?"

I beamed at him.

"I need to go home to fetch that story sack. It's finished and I was meant to return it this morning."

"Guess how much I love you?" Scott asked.

"As far as the moon?" I answered shyly, knowing he'd read the book earlier, while I was changing.

"To the moon, AND back!" he answered. "And from now on, I'm going to make sure I show you, and Alex, how much I do love you."

First published in *The People's Friend* in March 2005

All She Had to Give

The sooner it was out of the way, the better, really, Jeanne thought. She knew it was going to be a hard job and had packed a box of tissues into an already over-flowing wicker basket.

"Do you want a hand, dear?" a voice asked from behind her.

Jeanne stiffened. She definitely didn't want anyone offering to take or sort out any of her mum's treasured possessions.

"That's very kind of you… Edith, isn't it? But I'll manage," Jeanne replied as politely as she could.

"I'm just next door if you need me, dear. The kettle's always on, remember," the old woman continued kindly. She looked frail but her voice was strong.

Jeanne had met Edith a few times before when she'd been visiting her mum but they'd only ever passed the time of day.

"My mother told me about you," Jeanne began slowly, trying to remember in what context it had been.

"We played Scrabble," Edith supplied helpfully.

"Oh yes!" Jeanne exclaimed. "Mum was so pleased that you'd included her in your little group. It meant a lot to her that you all made her feel welcome, especially when she first moved in."

"We really enjoyed her company and hearing about you and how skilled you are at flower arranging! She'll be sadly missed."

Jeanne unlocked the door to her mother's home, smiling at Edith as the old woman turned to go indoors and thought that perhaps she would take her up on that cup of tea later.

Jeanne avoided looking at all the photos in the stillness of the living-room and made straight for her mother's bedroom.

She unravelled a black bin liner from the roll and began to fill it up.

After a while, she went to the kitchen and disposed of an assortment of rusty cake tins and food past its sell-by date.

By midday, Jeanne felt much better. She'd cleared a lot already. Yet so far, she'd not shed a single tear. She'd kept herself busy, not allowing herself to think too deeply about what she was doing, and why.

Jeanne had arranged to have lunch today in the restaurant of the housing complex and, during the course of her meal, a couple of residents came over to offer their condolences. Her mother obviously had been well known and even more popular than she'd imagined. It made her feel glad that her mother had been in such friendly surroundings during her final years.

Jeanne had been against the move here, thinking that it would be too stressful for her mother to sell the much-loved family home, although she'd admitted it was too big.

However, her mother had sold up and, with the proceeds, had bought a two-bedroomed ground-floor flat in these beautiful, sheltered surroundings.

There was always a warden on site, and staff on hand to help with all sorts of things, if necessary.

"I'm so sorry about your mother," another lady, who leant on her Zimmer frame and smiled, interrupted Jeanne's thoughts. "I don't know what I'll do with all my jars now!"

"Jam jars?" Jeanne asked uncertainly. She had a brief, but highly embarrassing vision of her mother surrounded by old jam jars – still with the labels on them – crammed full of flowers. It wasn't as if she didn't have plenty of perfectly good crystal and China vases but she'd always put the flowers Jeanne brought into any containers, suitable or otherwise, that she could find.

Jeanne shuddered at the thought. She'd never live it down if the flower club ever found out.

"I don't know what she did with them. Storage, I think," the woman added as she gripped the Zimmer again and went on her way.

Puzzled, Jeanne returned to the flat to do some more clearing out.

On getting there, she was glad to see that the cardboard boxes she'd asked for, had arrived and were stacked outside the flat. Bit by bit, she loaded these with items she wanted to keep and things for the next jumble sale.

While she was sorting out, she did notice that her mother, bless her, had stuck labels underneath one or two of the more valuable pieces. One label said, *For John, because he took me out on my birthday.* Another said, *For Rosie, who rang me every day when I had 'flu.*

At least that makes my job easier, Jeanne realised. She then came across a familiar chipped China bowl. The label underneath said, *For Jeanne, for her flower arranging... She always liked it...*

Jeanne smiled remembering her childhood fascination with the little flowers and butterflies which decorated it. She'd almost forgotten it, but her mother hadn't...

She chuckled a little at the image of the old bowl taking pride of place in a flower arranging competition. Then the tears came to her eyes and the long-forgotten bowl became suddenly precious.

By the end of the day, the flat was spick and span. It was more or less empty, too. Jeanne decided on one last look round. One thing was still bothering her. Where were the jam jars? Jeanne double-checked the lounge, bathroom, spare bedroom then her mother's bedroom again. All were empty.

The last job on her list was to read the meters to settle their accounts. When she pulled open the meter cupboard, it was like a fruit machine giving out a jackpot – there must have been twenty or more jam jars packed full with coins and notes.

The jars were neatly labelled with people's names. Inside were varying amounts. Her mother, apparently, had put a pound in the appropriate jar, every time someone had done her a kindness – when someone visited, rang, sent a card, or ran an errand – to show her appreciation.

Jeanne's own jar was right at the front and was full of short notes and little cards, written by her mother, telling Jeanne how much she loved her and what a wonderful, caring daughter she'd always been.

Happy tears sprang to Jeanne's eyes at her mother's loving words. Her mother had always said she was grateful but Jeanne had frequently felt guilty that she'd not done enough for her – not been there as often as she should, not spent enough time with her.

Now, she realised, that was just her grief talking. Her mother had been delighted with her attentiveness. Now she could let these guilty feelings go and only remember instead the many happy, special times they'd shared over the years.

For these memories truly were the greatest riches of all.

Originally published in *My weekly* in April 2003

Beside the Seaside

Britain 1920

"My goodness Enid, you are chipper this morning," his Lordship said. He was reading his newspaper in the library while Enid was clearing the grate.

"Shall I come back later Sir?" she asked.

"No, that's not necessary, you carry on." He seemed somewhat flustered. "But please refrain from singing."

"Sorry Sir, I had no idea I was doing it." Enid did a little curtsey and then returned to her chores.

After only a few minutes, he folded his newspaper, sat back and crossed his legs.

"Come here Enid," he said.

Enid stood, brushed down her apron and presented herself. The Master studied her for a moment or two, and then smiled.

"So, what's got into you?" he asked. "You seem full of the joys of spring. Have you met a young man?"

"Oh no, Sir." Enid was shocked by his suggestion.

"What's put you in such a good mood then?" Enid looked down at her second-hand boots.

"Come on girl, I want to know, because I've been in Italy for a month which was supposed to cheer me up, but it didn't do the trick."

"I'm sorry Sir, didn't you have a good holiday then?"

"It took simply ages to get there, and when we arrived, the place was too hot and too dusty. The food tasted odd, even the water didn't agree with her Ladyship. No one spoke a word of English, and by the time the newspapers arrived; they were at least a day late."

"Sorry to hear that, Sir."

"I seem to remember you had a week with your aunt; was that a better experience?"

"Oh, I had a wonderful time Sir,"

"Wonderful? How?" he asked her. "What was so good about it?"

"Well, Sir, it felt so good to breathe in the sea air; sometimes you can taste the salt on your lips. I ate fresh fish every day, I sat on a donkey and I borrowed my cousin's bathing suit and went in the sea. It was freezing, but somehow it felt good. I felt alive! If you know what I mean, Sir?"

"Oh dear, so now I suppose you'd like to go and live by the seaside?"

"Oh no, Sir," Enid was quick to tell him. "Truly, I had the best time, but it was even better to come home."

"I too was glad to get home," his Lordship agreed.

"I better get on Sir, or Mrs Winter won't be pleased, she'll have my guts for garters, she will!"

Enid hurriedly finished clearing the grate, and made up the fire ready to be lit.

Meanwhile, Lord Henley stood and stared out of the large bay window into the distance. Nothing was quite the same since the Great War, and now they had the Spanish flu to contend with. No wonder it was harder to recruit, and then to keep staff, both inside the manor and on the estate.

"Is everything all right?" Lady Henley asked as she entered the room. "You look as though you've got the world on your shoulders."

"I want to expand the farm, to try new crops and rear more cattle, but we've barely got enough workers to manage what we have now."

"It's the same for me," Lady Henley told him. "Daisy has been acting as Lady's Maid but, quite frankly, she's much more suited to the scullery. Servants are so hard to come by now-a-days." She sighed. "It was so different before the war; we had people queuing up for work and they were all so loyal. Nanny stayed for three generations!"

Downstairs Enid was set to polish the footwear that the family had brought back from their month in Europe.

"I've never seen so many pairs of shoes. I only have these boots, and those are hand-me-downs."

Mr Reed was busy polishing the master's riding boots. Enid told him of her strange conversation with his Lordship.

"I don't know why they bothered to go, if you ask me," Mr Reed the footman said. "From what I hear, they wanted Cook to do the same meals she prepares here, which was really difficult, because it was hard to get some of the ingredients. They didn't leave the house they were staying in because it was too hot outside. They didn't entertain any guests. Her Ladyship worked on her tapestry and His Lordship read old newspapers and complained about the insects and the unsavoury smells."

"His Lordship didn't seem to enjoy himself," Enid admitted. "I felt awful bad telling him what a wonderful time I'd had." At this, Mr Reed raised an eyebrow. "He asked me what was so good about my holiday!"

Empire Day was fast approaching on 24th May and Lady Henley had been considering whether she ought to give the servants a half day in recognition of their hard work, and their loyalty.

"The trouble is," she confessed to Lord Henley. "I don't know what we would do without them."

Lord Henley carefully folded his newspaper and looked at his wife. "I do have an idea," he said. "I recently read an article about a company who were losing their workers to a competitor, so they arranged a day out for their employees. It was a great success and they've since made it an annual event. Needless to say, they've not only retained their staff, but morale has increased."

"I don't really see the connection," began Lady Henley.

"I'm suggesting we hire a carriage or a charabanc and take the entire household to the seaside for the day. I think the fresh sea air would do us all some good."

At that point, Enid came in with their tray of tea.

"You recently stayed with your aunt on the coast?" he asked her. She nodded. "Can you tell her Ladyship and me, what you enjoyed most?"

"The taste of the fish and chips; the sea breeze in my hair; the feel of the sand between my toes; hearing the sound of the gulls, the…"

"Thank you, Enid," her Ladyship said. "I can tell you had the most wonderful time."

"Oh, I did, your Ladyship. I love visiting my aunt, but it's nice to come home, where I belong."

Lord Henley waited until Enid had left the room before addressing his wife, "Didn't you see the way her face lit up? I've never seen her so animated."

"Indeed," her Ladyship conceded, "she certainly seemed to enjoy herself; but can we trust them to come back?"

"That's why I feel we ought to accompany them. Obviously, we would have our own transport and I've heard of a very pleasant hotel where one can take tea and have a good view of the pleasure beach, without actually having to venture down to the water."

"It's good to hear you enthuse about something," Lady Henley told him. "You've been so melancholy lately."

Almost as soon as the day trip was announced, Lord Henley became aware of the change of atmosphere in the manor.

Lady Henley was careful to show more of an interest in the menu Cook had suggested for the servant's picnic, and confided in him that Daisy, her usually dour lady's maid, had been caught smiling!

Fortunately, the sun shone as the charabanc pulled up outside the manor house. Lord Henley watched from the drawing room window; he hardly recognised some of them, dressed in their Sunday Best.

In order to allow their chauffeur to join in the festivities, he'd volunteered to drive Lady Henley and himself, in his new open top motor car. In fact, he was looking forward to getting behind the wheel, even more than breathing the sea air.

Lord Henley thoroughly enjoyed the sense of freedom he got from driving himself on a beautiful sunny day. He was thankful his wife entered into the spirit of things, and had bought a new outfit especially for the occasion.

It had been arranged she should meet with her sister and their niece at The Grand Hotel which overlooked the sea. Lord Henley gave them the opportunity to talk while he took himself for a walk, promising to return for luncheon.

Lord Henley strolled along the front, past a very ornate promenade shelter. He could hear the gulls which Enid had spoken of, but in the distance he also heard music. A band was playing.

To him, this was a world of colour, so unlike the wood panelled library where he spent the majority of his time, nor the stuffy boardroom where he had to sit and listen to boring speeches, or the crisp white tablecloths of his favourite restaurant.

He spotted Enid. She was standing on the sand with her boots in one hand. She seemed mesmerised by a children's puppet show. One puppet, dressed in red and yellow, was intent on hitting another.

Lord Henley paused at a stall selling bright pink Seaside Rock. He bought four sticks; one for his wife, his sister-in-law, his niece and himself. As he left, he realised he would never have entered the tobacconist's in the village to buy confectionary, but here, just for the day, it felt different.

He saw Enid looking at straw hats.

"It wouldn't suit you," he said, making her jump. "Are you enjoying your day?" he asked.

"I most certainly am, Sir," Enid replied, giving a little curtsey.

"You realise, this is all down to you?"

"Me Sir?"

"Yes, if you hadn't been so damn cheerful after your holiday, I would never have considered this outing."

Enid looked down at her bare feet. She was still carrying her boots.

They strolled along the promenade. "May I treat you to an ice cream, as a thank you?" Lord Henley asked.

"I shouldn't really Sir," Enid said. "Cook's prepared the most marvellous picnic."

"I too have luncheon to return to," he confessed, "but they do look rather tempting." He smiled at Enid and she grinned when Lord Henley approached the Ice cream seller.

"It'll have to be our secret," he told her as he handed Enid a little pot of the cold dessert.

"Delicious," Enid said as she licked the creamy white ice-cream. His Lordship heartily agreed, although he knew his wife would be horrified to know he was eating something on the street!

"Now run along Enid and enjoy the picnic," he said,

dismissing her. He watched her carrying her boots by their laces and thought how you could do things beside the seaside, that you would never entertain doing whilst at home. Things like going barefoot, or eating a dessert on the pavement! He smiled, enjoying his liberty.

As much as Lord Henley had enjoyed venturing out along the promenade, he was pleased to be back in The Grand Hotel and to be seated in a quiet dining hall with his wife and her family. They were politely grateful for the stick of seaside rock.

"If nothing else, it will serve as a reminder of today," he laughed. "You don't really have to try it."

After luncheon Lord Henley was surprised to hear his wife request a short stroll around the hotel gardens so she could breathe in the sea air, hear the gulls and understand what all the fuss was about.

"I think I'll join you," he said and offered her his arm.

"These gardens are delightful," Lady Henley said as she admired several of the plants and small trees she'd never seen before. "Would a seaside garden work at home?"

All too soon, it was time to head back to the comfort of the manor. Lord Henley's motor car followed the charabanc for part of the journey. They could hear them singing and congratulated themselves on a successful day.

"I'd say that was quite a triumph," Lord Henley declared.

"I too admit to feeling invigorated by the sea air," agreed Lady Henley. "It's a shame we no longer have a team of gardeners. I really cannot see Timpson having the time to make me a seaside garden, when he has the kitchen garden to tend."

"In that case, we'll have to make an annual pilgrimage to the coast, so you can breathe the sea air and wander amongst the palm trees."

“That would be delightful, and I am sure it will boost our servants’ morale. From now on, this is how we’ll celebrate Empire Day; with a jolly day by the seaside.”

First published in *The People’s Friend 2024 Annual*, on sale Summer 2023

Be Careful What You Wish For

"I just love everything about Rome!" Mary said. "I'm so happy I feel I could dance all night." Mary linked her arm through Joe's and tried to get him to skip along with her.

They walked past an ornate stone fountain and entered a Trattoria. Inside it was dark and cosy with wooden furniture, no plastic in sight! The tables were dressed with red and white gingham tablecloths and candles flickered, adding the feeling of warmth. Italian folk guitar music played in the background. Joe smiled at the pretty Italian waitress who showed them to their table.

"It was a lot cheaper twenty-five years ago," he moaned as they looked at the menu.

"We were young and poor in those days, now we've got good jobs, a healthy bank balance and some savings," Mary reminded him.

"Not if we keep having weekends away in five-star hotels,"

"Last month it was my 50th and now it's our Silver Wedding Anniversary. I think they're both worth celebrating. I thought you did too."

"But Munster are at home this weekend," joked Joe – an armchair fan. He shut his menu and Mary suspected he'd opt for spaghetti bolognaise because it was familiar and cheap.

"Munster were at home the day we married, and I seem to remember they won. I'm sure it was part of Dad's speech. Maeve promised she'd record the rugby for you, so you won't miss a thing."

"It's not the same as watching it live. There's no atmosphere when you know the result."

"There's nothing we can do about it now. I'm very grateful for the ultimate sacrifice you've made by bringing me here. Now do let's try and enjoy it." Mary pecked him on the cheek.

It was still barmy as they left the restaurant about an hour later. Mary breathed in the warm Italian air and danced along the road, trying to get Joe to join in.

"Let's go for a walk," Mary linked her arm through his. "I know you don't like spending money, but I'm so glad we've come here. It's so beautiful and it's not as if we can't afford a treat once in a while. It was a good deal and we haven't had a holiday in years." She reached up and kissed him lightly on the cheek. "Thank you for booking it. You've made me very happy. Now we just need you to forget the stresses of work, and lighten up a bit."

They strolled down old streets, passed one ancient building after another until they reached an open square, near their hotel, with yet another huge fountain in the centre.

"Let's make a wish," said Mary smiling at another couple who had stopped at the fountain. She opened her beaded evening bag for a coin.

"Save your money if I were you," said a voice that could have been Joe's, it was that cranky! Mary thought she'd recognised the couple from the hotel.

"Simon!" said the woman next to him. "I'm sorry, he's an old misery guts; don't take any notice of him." Mary smiled. It seems they all turn into grumpy old men when they reach a certain age. Despite that, Mary knew Joe loved her, and they'd both be lost without each other.

She smiled back at them, picked a coin from her purse and threw it into the fountain. It made a ripple in the cold water and sank to the bottom, along with a small fortune of foreign currency. Why don't they empty it, she wondered? Mary briefly closed her eyes and made her wish.

"I wouldn't if I were you," warned Simon again. "Wishes can be dangerous. Sometimes they come true. You're playing with fire."

"Simon!" said his wife again as she led him briskly back toward the hotel.

"Aren't you going to wish?" Mary asked as she looked up at Joe. He was still a handsome man, even though his hair had changed over the years from black to grey to white.

At that moment her mobile hummed in her bag. It was a message from their daughter.

"Goodness!" Mary said beaming from ear to ear, her eyes twinkling with excitement. "That man was right. I'd just been wishing how wonderful it would be, to be grandparents, and now Maeve's sent me a photo of her positive pregnancy test. She and Paul wanted to tell us in person, but couldn't wait until we got home."

"More expense," moaned Joe but there was a flicker of a smile.

Mary let out an exaggerated sigh. She loved him, but sometimes wondered where the man she'd married, had gone. Never one to give up, she gave his arm an affectionate little squeeze. "It's the best thing I've heard in ages. And you know you'll love being a grandfather. It makes my life complete," she grinned. She looked around for someone to share her news with. Already, she was buzzing with ideas of baby-clothes to knit. Suddenly she was full of questions for her daughter, had they thought of names? Did they want to know the sex of the child beforehand? And, most importantly, was she feeling, ok? As much as Mary was enjoying their mini-break, she now felt torn; she wanted to be with her daughter, check she was eating properly and taking enough rest.

Joe was still looking at the fountain. The stone angel looked down on him as if waiting impatiently for his small change.

"Shall we go back to the hotel for a coffee? Or a drink, to celebrate? We could tell that couple our news, or are you going to make a wish?" Mary offered him a Euro.

Joe heaved a sigh. "I'll wish, if it will stop you nagging me!" He stood up straight, and, taking the Euro said with a grin, "I wish for a wife thirty years younger than me!"

As he leaned forward to throw the coin, something went "ping" in his back. He gasped and bent double. He yelped in agony and wriggled in pain.

"For goodness sake Joe, one mention of you being a grandpa and now you're acting like an octogenarian!" Despite her teasing, Mary put her arm gently round him. Joe gave her a rare smile.

"Why do you put up with me?" he asked.

"I sometimes ask myself that, but every so often I get a glimpse of the man I married, and that keeps me going."

Joe went pale and grabbed the railing round the edge of the fountain.

"It's no joke. I do feel like an eighty-year-old." He rubbed his back and muttered, "That guy was right. You've got to be careful what you wish for. I foolishly wished for a wife thirty years younger, and it appears that's what I've got!"

Mary rolled her eyes. "Aren't you pleased with their news?" she asked seriously. Joe rubbed his back, then took her hand in his and kissed it tenderly.

"You know me, I'm an old softy really." He turned his head and Mary wondered if he was wiping away a tear. "I just want to be fit and active enough to run around after a toddler – I hear they can be exhausting!"

"Well," Mary said. "I've only got one coin left. You better be really careful what you wish for this time."

In The Groove

It was against all the rules to have a first date with a stranger, in their own home BUT I only went ahead because Fredrik shared a flat with my best friend Anna and her sister.

I rang his door bell dead on seven thirty as he'd asked. It was Anna who opened the door.

"Don't worry I won't chaperone you all evening but I shall be popping in and out to the kitchen and it's all open plan."

I felt relieved. I'd had a long-term relationship which had fallen apart years ago and it had taken me ages to pick myself up, but now I was ready to enjoy some male company.

"Come and meet Fredrik," she'd said. "He's a bit eccentric but his heart is in the right place."

It was a welcome distraction. We were having, yet another, "restructure" at work. There will be more job losses. I'd survived so far because I work hard but there's only so much uncertainty you can have. It takes its toll.

I caught a whiff of aftershave. It made me smile that someone had gone to the trouble of wearing aftershave, for me. I liked that.

Fredrik was tall and broad whereas I was slight and skinny, but they say opposites attract, so who knows?

I'd intended to stick with coffee to keep a clear head but there was a bottle of red wine open with two glasses on a tray. I felt I needed a drink to give me courage. "Just a small one," I said.

Fredrik poured the wine, only half a glass. I was glad he'd listened to me. He carried the tray into the lounge area and chose the chair while I sat at right angles to him on the sofa.

We chatted a bit about ourselves, what work we did and so on and then the conversation dried up. I think he was about as nervous as I was. I desperately looked around for inspiration and found it in the form of an old-fashioned record player.

"Do you like music?" I asked nodding at the turntable. His eyes lit up and I knew I'd done the right thing.

"What's your taste in music?" he asked and opened up a cupboard to reveal his extensive record collection. "Let me see," Fredrik said as he looked firstly at me, as if it was only now, that he'd registered my existence, and then thoughtfully back to his vast collection. I wondered what he'd seen in me, and what he'd choose.

I was fascinated. He seemed to have an idea in mind and somehow plucked it from the shelf. I have to admit, even with my glasses on all the album spines looked the same to me.

He handed me a pair of headphones and said, "Lie, sit, stretch out, whatever suits you. Eyes open or closed, you'll know what's best."

With that Fredrik put on his own headphones and lay down on the rug on his back with his eyes closed. I was surprised how nimble he was and found myself wondering if he danced.

I had been sitting on the edge of the sofa almost bolt upright, not letting myself be caught off guard. Was I really that anxious about this date?

Suddenly David Cassidy's *How Can I Be Sure?* filled my ears. I reached out for a couple of cushions to stuff behind me so I could relax back into them and without really being aware, closed my eyes and let the song take me back to 1972.

Amazingly the words were just as poignant all these years later. "How can I be sure in a world that's constantly changing?"

Next Fredrik chose Elton John's *Rocket Man* from about the same era.

The third song on his playlist was Gilbert O'Sullivan's *Alone Again, naturally* and those words brought me back to reality. Was I going to be on my own for the rest of my life?

But… there were times when I wanted to discuss a film or share a meal or have a hug.

I opened my eyes and saw Fredrik stretched out like a huge Blue Whale and wondered – gentle giant though he was, was he the man for me? There had been no spark… yet, but I'd always be in his debt because he'd re-introduced me to music which had been decidedly absent in my life.

Fredrik must have sensed my movement as I rearranged the cushions propping me up.

"Not your taste?" he asked in surprise.

"You were spot on," I told him and his whole face lit up again. I wouldn't say he was handsome but his was a friendly face, one I could get used to.

I was grateful when Anna appeared and made herself a coffee. She looked in my direction and I smiled.

"More seventies?" Fredrik asked.

"She's got an empty wine glass," Anna called. "I'd fill it first if I were you."

"Actually, I'd like a coffee please and something upbeat. I need cheering up. I could go in to work tomorrow to be told I've been made redundant after seventeen years with them."

"Something bright and cheerful," Fredrik muttered.

"It's a double-edged sword really. Even if I go in and find I've got my job, someone else will be clearing their desk and I'll go home feeling guilty."

I didn't think Fredrik had really listened to me when he chose a violinist and his orchestra to cheer me up. The LP cover looked almost modern. I began to think of ways to make my excuses and head for home.

I'd not discovered Andre Rieu and his orchestra until that moment. It only took one track before I was hooked. I had tears rolling down my cheeks because of the way he'd made that violin sing. I was happy to listen to the rest of the album and, for the first time in ages, I kicked off my shoes and lay back on the sofa sipping coffee and got into the groove.

"Thank you so much," I said again. It had been the weirdest date ever but just what I needed. I knew I had to get home, have a good night's rest and face tomorrow. However, I now felt that whatever happened I could face the music and move on. Life had all been about work. It was time to redress the balance and introduce song and dance back into my world. Fredrik and his music had given me the strength to accept what I couldn't change.

First published in *Allas*, Sweden in August 2019

The Promise

I liked Sam as soon as I saw him. I think the attraction was mutual.

We both lived in a high-rise block on the twelfth floor. I often saw him on the stairs. He always seemed to be in training, and so never used the lift. Whenever I saw him, he was wearing his fluorescent cycling gear, making him easy to spot.

"I don't suppose you could do me a huge favour?" he asked one morning as I was off to work. "I'm doing a triathlon in a few weeks, and I've got no one to look after Jamie."

My heart sank. To me, Jamie sounded like a small child. I hadn't got him down as a single dad.

"You're wise not to agree until you've met her. Come round tonight for a glass of wine and I'll introduce you."

"Should you be drinking wine if you're in training?" I said before I could stop myself. I was sounding like my mother.

"I'm on water, but I could hardly ask you over for a glass of water, now, could I? Seven o'clock, okay? I'm the one with the blue door."

"Okay, I'll call round then."

By eight o'clock that evening and after two glasses of wine I was wishing Jamie had been his daughter.

Jamie, I soon realised was a much loved, and very spoilt parrot. That is, Sam adored his pet, but unfortunately Jamie and I took an instant dislike to each other.

Ridiculous as it sounds, she made me feel as though I was *the other woman.*

Sam talked me through his evening routine. He checked all the windows were closed, then drew the curtains and covered the mirror, before opening the cage and letting Jamie fly around.

I was out of my comfort zone having a large parrot flying around in a confined space, but agreed it did her good as she was shut up in the cage all day and this was the only exercise she got.

Once Jamie was back in her cage, Sam went through how to feed her. She ate mainly seeds and nuts with some fresh fruit which Sam promised to stock up with before he went.

By the time he'd shown me what size to cut up her grapes and how to administer her vitamins, I'd finished another glass of wine.

I saw Sam most days after that. I can't say we ever went out on a date because we had to work around his very strict training schedule. He lived on rabbit food, didn't drink alcohol and couldn't have late nights. He did promise to take me out properly, once his triathlon was over.

I waved him off at the station and held his key in my hand. Jamie was due to be let out for her exercise in under an hour so I had to hurry home.

Carefully I checked and then doubled checked the windows. I might not be a fan of caged birds but I didn't want Jamie escaping. I remembered to close the curtains so she didn't see her reflection in the glass and get confused. Then I gingerly unhooked the cage door.

Jamie just sat there, looking at me. I stepped back to allow her more freedom but we continued to stare at each other.

Then suddenly she shot out of the cage and headed straight for me. It all happened so quickly.

She swerved at the last minute, flying behind me and into the wall. There was a loud thump. It was then I remembered I hadn't covered the mirror. She'd obviously seen her reflection and crashed into it.

I'd only been in Sam's flat fifteen minutes and already I was regretting it.

I was as stunned as the parrot for a few seconds, but soon came to my senses. Anxiously I checked she was still breathing and then rang my brother.

I never thought I'd be so pleased to have an intelligent sibling who was training to be a vet.

"So, can you help?" I asked having described what had just happened.

"Hayley, I'm in my first term. You might be surprised to know it, but we haven't covered concussed parrots yet. But, don't worry I'll be over pronto."

I couldn't just wait for Jake. I carefully lifted Jamie and put her on a cushion on the floor. I didn't want her to come to and then fall off the cabinet.

I'd noticed there was a Tupperware box in the kitchen labelled "Jamie's Treats". It seemed to be full of plain biscuits. I broke one in half and carried it into the lounge.

The biscuit worked like smelling salts. One whiff of digestive and Jamie perked up. She did look a bit wobbly but I wasn't taking any chances. I gently scooped her up and returned her to the cage locking the little door with a huge sigh of relief.

Jake arrived soon after.

"Do you want me to examine her?" he asked.

"Under no circumstances are you to open the cage. If I've learnt anything tonight it's that I shall never, ever, offer to look after someone's pet ever again."

Jake peered in at her but then started to giggle.

"What's so funny?" I asked. My hands were still shaking and I felt sick at the thought of what might have happened.

"On my way here, I Googled 'concussed parrots'," he told me, and my heart went out to my heroic brother, but he continued. "Have you ever seen the Monty Python Dead Parrot Sketch?"

Before I knew it, he'd got it up on his phone. I tried not to laugh but gave in.

"Just promise you'll never tell Sam," I said and wiped the tears away where I'd been laughing so much.

"Just promise you'll never tell Sam," echoed Jamie again and again.

"A talking African Grey, well I never," said Jake in admiration, while I glared at her. She'd never once opened her mouth before, and Sam hadn't mentioned she could speak or mimic.

"Just promise you'll never tell Sam." Repeated Jamie.

"She's very good," Jake said with a silly grin. "She's got your voice down to a tee. Perfect."

"Just promise you'll never tell Sam." Announced Jamie yet again as I switched off the light and realised that was the end of my relationship with Sam, and what's more, Jamie knew it. She'd won.

First published in *Allas*, Sweden in July 2018

Waiting for the Wedding

"When are you going to make an honest woman of the girl?" Grandpa asked Tom.

"I keep asking, but she won't have me."

"Really?" his grandpa said.

"You've been together for years. What's the problem?"

Tom took a deep breath and sat at the kitchen table. He put his head in his hands.

"It's so stupid really," he began. "About five years ago we went to her best friend's wedding. She was a bridesmaid."

"Pink dress?" Gran nodded to herself as though she were picturing the photo.

"That's right." Tom smiled at the memory. "Well, at the reception there was this weird woman. Tall and thin with long red hair and nails to match. She was part of the band; she played saxophone."

His grandparents looked at each other and back at Tom.

"We were all sitting down after the speeches and this woman looked straight at Liz and said, 'It's no use marrying him, it won't work.' "

"Silly woman," Grandpa said. "What does she know?"

"Exactly!" echoed Tom. "I keep telling Liz that. The woman had never met us. She'd probably argued with her own boyfriend and was feeling miserable."

"But Liz believed what she said?" Gran asked quietly. Tom nodded and looked down at his ring-less hands.

Two months later Liz was sitting at the corner table in the café waiting for Tom. He was late which wasn't like him but it had been pouring all day; maybe the main road had been flooded again?

The café door chimed as a tall redhead made her entrance. Her coat dripped puddles as she wriggled out of it and headed straight for the corner table… and Liz.

Liz recognised her at once from Becky's wedding. She was filled with doom and gloom. Had something dreadful happened to Tom?

"Don't worry," the woman said. "I shan't stay long." Nevertheless she slid into the chair opposite Liz. "I don't know if you remember me,"

"I do," Liz told her. "And I don't think we have anything to say to each other."

"Well, you're wrong there," the woman wiped raindrops from her forehead. "I'll be honest with you. I can't remember exactly what I said. I meet loads of people and sometimes I pick up vibes or get a feeling and I feel it's my duty to say something."

"And ruin their lives?"

"You didn't have to listen… or take me seriously,"

"It was too late for that. You'd already put a curse on our relationship telling us it would never work."

The woman turned to face Liz. "I'm sorry for what I said. And even more upset that you took it to heart. If the truth be told I have a lot of premonitions, but I never follow them up to see whether I was right… or not. It's not like I'm on Trip Advisor and people can leave a review. I must have picked up on something negative that day,"

"The bride and groom split up last year,"

"Well perhaps that was it, who knows, maybe I'd had too much to drink? But I'm stone cold sober now and I'm telling you to forget it. Understand?"

"Has he told you to say this?" Liz asked.

"Better than that, he paid me!" The woman slapped a brown envelope down on the table.

Liz bit her lip. What did he think he was playing at? "I think you've said more than enough. Please go."

The redhead stood and reached for her sopping wet coat. "I will tell you something for nothing. I've moved house four times since that wedding and changed my name. It must have taken quite a bit of detective work for him to track me down. I think that anyone who goes to that much trouble must be crazy about you. Just think about it."

With that the woman slid the envelope across the table toward Liz. "I can't take his money. He's done me a favour. I've always assumed people want their fortunes told and I never charge, but now I'll ask first before I jump in. Put the money toward the wedding."

With that the woman disappeared. Liz looked up from the brown envelope lying on the café table. Tom was standing there with a ring in his hand. She hadn't even noticed him arrive.

"I won't embarrass you by going down on one knee if the answer's still no," he said quietly.

Liz looked at his dripping, tousled hair. She wanted to run her fingers through it and kiss his damp lips.

"Try me," she said.

As if in slow motion, Tom got down on one knee much to the interest of the entire café.

"Marry me, Liz? I can't tell you how much I love you. Please say yes."

The woman's words re-played in her head. "Anyone who goes to that much trouble must be crazy about you."

"Yes," she whispered.

The customers cheered. Tom slipped the ring on her finger and kissed her forehead. As if from nowhere his grandparents appeared carrying a bottle of fizz and four glasses! The curse had been broken.

First published in the *My Weekly 2023 Annual* on sale in September 2022. (Original title was "The Wedding Curse", hence the last line.)

Fridays with Mum

It was Friday, and I never knew what to expect when I went to visit Mum. We've always been close, even more so since we lost Dad. In fact, that's why Simon and I split up. He was jealous of Mum! He said I was more eager to see her, than him. As soon as he accused me, I realised it was true, and that was the end of my relationship with Simon. He could be a bit possessive.

"Hi," I said, leaning over and pecking Mum on the cheek. She looked a bit pale, but her eyes were twinkling.

"Hello Julie love. You're looking pretty today. I like you in that top."

"Thanks," I said, pleased she'd noticed I'd made an effort. I'd got into the habit of wearing tatty jeans. "What have you got in store for us today? A Garden Centre?"

"I've got an appointment," she said. "I hope you don't mind. It shouldn't take long. And I thought about a Macmillan Coffee Morning afterwards?"

"Good thinking," I told her. About a year ago, we'd all had some intensive training at work. It was meant to ensure employees made better use of our time, be more productive by knowing how to prioritise. The course backfired, instead of making me work harder; I realised that spending time with Mum was my main priority and so I asked to change my hours and work only four days a week. It's great not working Fridays, because I always have a lovely long weekend, and I go back to work on Monday feeling refreshed. Perhaps the woman who ran the course did know her stuff, after all?

Mum's not been 100% these last few months. A routine mammogram showed a shadow, which was probably nothing, but they removed it anyway. Then, just to be sure, she's got some new follow-up "treatment".

We were in luck today and found a parking space outside the clinic. The sun was shining, and it promised to be a beautiful day.

"Now," Mum said, turning to look at me, rather than immediately getting out of the car. My heart sank. "You're not to worry, this is just a precaution."

"What am I not meant to worry about?" I asked her with a tremble in my voice.

"We're going to visit Wendy The Wig," Mum said. "The Doctor said I probably won't lose my hair, but if I do, I'd like to be prepared."

"Oh,"

"Come on, it could be fun." Having said her piece, she picked up her bag, and got out of the car. She gave me a grin. "I've been looking forward to this."

I'm always amazed how wonderfully positive she is; some people make more fuss about going to the dentist.

We checked in at reception and the nurse said Wendy's last appointment was running a little late, but she shouldn't keep us too long.

"Is she really called Wendy The Wig?" I whispered to Mum as we waited.

"Of course," Mum smiled. "What did you think she'd be called, Flick?"

"Married to a man called Bob?" We laughed. I wanted to remind her of a hairdresser we'd seen on holiday called "Curl up and Dye" but somehow, I just couldn't get the words out.

"Wendy's free now," the receptionist told us. "The Hair Salon's just down that corridor, you'll see it, right at the end."

Mum stood and gathered her belongings. She'd worn her best coat and a scarf I'd given her for her last birthday, along with new shoes that matched her handbag. It comforted me that she was still taking an interest in the way she looked. It gave me hope. It also made me put on smart trousers, instead of my old jeans.

I remained seated. Sometimes she wanted me to go in with her to these appointments, but at other times she'd decide to go alone. Today I'd brought my iPad along, thinking I might pluck up the courage to join a dating site. It had been over a year since I'd broken up with Simon. I'd made the most of having time to myself, but now I was ready for some masculine company.

"Come on Julie," Mum said. "I need you to tell me what you think."

We headed on down the corridor and sure enough, facing us was a Hair Salon that wouldn't have looked out of place on the high street. It was aptly named, "Cutting it Fine".

We entered, chuckling at the name. Wendy The Wig, greeted us. She wore a nursing uniform, which was to be expected, but her hair was elegantly arranged in a French pleat and her face was perfectly made up. She looked as glamorous as Trixie in *Call the Midwife*. Her manner was efficient and professional.

Having checked a few basics with Mum, she led us from the waiting area into her studio. The walls were lined with shelves stacked with a selection of boxes. Some were circular, more like hat boxes, which seemed appropriate, while others resembled shoe boxes.

Wendy sat my Mum down in a swivel chair in front of a large mirror. The room had probably been an outdoor store cupboard at one time, but now there was a pitched glass roof flooding the room with light.

"Let me look at you," Wendy said as she gently ran her fingers through Mum's hair.

Everyone said Mum and I looked alike. I'd inherited her

curly brown locks, whereas my sister was blonde like Dad. As a teenager I'd spent hours straightening my hair which just went frizzy when it rained. I'd given up now, and accepted the natural wave.

I noticed how fine Mum's hair was nowadays. Hers was predominantly mousy-brown with strands of silver, grey and white, but not enough to call her grey. She still had a good head of hair, and that was a blessing. Her skin was flawless; it kept her looking younger than her years.

"So," Wendy said. "Is there something in particular you fancy? Or shall we start with something similar to your natural look?"

"I'd like something like my daughter's style," Mum replied and gestured in my direction. It was ironic really, as I fancied anything but what I've actually got. I'd always envied my blonde sister.

Wendy's boxes were organised by colour, then size and finally by length. The largest section was "Brunettes". What Mum needed was small and short.

"Ignore the plastic cap, that's just for hygienic reasons. We'd obviously take it off, if you were wearing it for real."

"I like that," Mum said as she stroked the glossy wig. "I look thirty years younger. Do you think we might be mistaken for sisters?"

"It does suit you," Wendy agreed, gently brushing Mum's new "hair". "Are you happy with that, or do you want to try something different? There's no rush. I have got one with a few grey highlights?"

"I'll stick with this, if I need it," Mum added. "I was told I'm unlikely to lose my hair, but to be ready, just in case."

"It's best to do it that way round," Wendy agreed as she reached for her paperwork. "I'll just note down the style and size, in case you do need it."

"Is your next appointment very soon?" I asked. Wendy looked at the clock.

"Not yet, there's plenty of time. Do you have a question?" Wendy asked, giving me her full attention, but I looked over at my mother.

"Mum, did you want to try something else, just for the fun of it, if we're not taking up too much time?" Mum couldn't hide her excitement.

"Well, my dad's side were all ginger, and I always wondered what it would be like to have red hair." Mum chuckled. "In fact, I thought my girls would end up auburn at the very least, but Julie's brunette like me and Martina's fair like her father."

Wendy turned to another shelf and started opening and closing boxes. "There's one in particular, I think you'd like. Ah, here it is." She smoothed it out and carefully placed it on Mum's head. In many ways it wasn't dissimilar from the one she'd chosen, but the colour was a mix of golden highlights. Reds, golds, coppers and the odd silver thread.

"Wow, that's stunning," I told her.

"It's a lovely wig," Mum agreed. "But it's not me. It's far too fashionable."

"What about going blonde?" I asked. "I've always fancied that."

It didn't take Wendy long to find a lovely ash blonde style, wavy like mine, but in a neater bob.

"No, that doesn't look right at all," Mum was quick to say. "My eyebrows are too dark. You can tell it's not my natural colour." Mum pulled it off and handed it to me. I didn't need to be asked twice. I'd been itching to try something on.

As I was looking over Mum's shoulder into the mirror and admiring my new look, there was a gentle tap on the door.

"Excuse me," Wendy said, "I just need to answer this, I've been waiting for some patient files."

"Sorry," the young man said as he hugged a large pile of buff folders. "They're quite heavy. Do you want me to put them down on your desk?"

"Great, thanks," Wendy said. "I was only expecting four." The handsome man laughed.

"I told them you'd notice," he chuckled. "You're in demand, it seems. I said I'm sure you'd fit them in."

"Come on love," Mum said. "Wendy's obviously busy. Thank you so much for your time."

"If you really want one, you can buy them online." Wendy said. "This brand is good. They tend to fit snugly. The last thing you want, is for it to blow away in the wind!"

"Thank you," I replied, as I carefully put down the blonde wig. I didn't really want it. It made me look so like Martina, my younger sister – the blue-eyed girl, slim and happily married, everything I wasn't. "It was good to try it, but it's probably a decent hair-cut I need."

Wendy handed Mum a card where she'd written down the wig details should they ever be required. "My phone number's on there. Give me a call, if you need to. I'll book an appointment to go through all the practicalities of washing it, and so on. Take care."

We walked back through the salon waiting area and into the corridor that led us back to the main reception. The lovely man with the files was there collecting up a box of paperwork.

"Oh, that's much better," he said, "the blonde wasn't right for you."

"Are you sure?" I'd been disappointed, because I'd foolishly thought, dyeing my hair could have solved my problems. Would I have been happier being blonde?

"Definitely prefer you as you are," he said with a cheery smile. "But I'd be more than happy to discuss it further, over a drink." He reached over for a notepad on the reception desk and scribbled down his details. "I'm Darren, give me a call."

"Er, thank you," I said, still suffering from shock. It felt like years since anyone had asked me out for a drink. "I'm Julie, and this is my Mum."

"Pleased to meet you both," he smiled again. A genuine beam. "Actually ladies, I'm due a coffee break, and we're raising money today for Macmillan Nurses. Will you join me?"

Originally published by *My Weekly* in September 2021

Never Too Old!

Lizzie stood up with the large horse chestnut in her hand. She was aware of the winter sun on her back and the feeling that someone was watching her.

"I'll have it, if you don't want it," said a male voice breaking into her thoughts and making her jump.

"It's beautiful," said Lizzie as she admired the shiny conker in the palm of her hand.

"It's a whopper!" said Graham moving closer. "Do you play conkers?"

"No," laughed Lizzie. "It must be sixty years since I did and then my brother always beat me."

"I'll have it if you don't want it," repeated Graham. This time he reached out his hand for the prize conker still in Lizzie's warm hand.

She looked down at it and then up at him. He had nice eyes and a friendly face.

"Why this one in particular?" she asked.

"Look at the size of it." Graham held out a hand full of medium sized conkers for her to compare.

"Aren't you a bit old to be playing conkers?" teased Lizzie.

"You're never too old for a bit of fun," replied Graham with a smile. "But actually, it's for my grandchildren." He looked wistful for a moment. "Alfie's 7 and Eve's 3. I can't believe it really how the time's gone. I've never actually met them, although I've seen loads of photos and I've talked to them on the computer, you know on Skype."

"Do they live far away?" asked Lizzie.

"New Zealand," he nodded. "But they're coming to visit me next week and I want to give them a great time. I want to show them good old Britain at its best, possibly an old-fashioned, rose-tinted picture of Britain, but all the best bits, none the less."

"Like when we were kids?" laughed Lizzie feeling as though she'd known Graham all her life. "Long, sunny days. Playing in the park with friends, and not coming home until you're hungry and then having good old-fashioned meals like shepherd's pie or lamb stew followed by tinned peaches with Carnation milk."

"Now you're making me hungry!" laughed Graham, "but that's exactly what I mean." He paused for a moment looking a bit serious. "Don't get me wrong, I love a pizza sometimes or to watch a DVD but I want to be the sort of Grandpa that builds tree houses and…"

"Plays conkers?" added Lizzie handing over the giant conker. "Your need is greater than mine."

"If you don't play, why are you collecting them?"

"I spread them around my little bungalow to keep the spiders away," Lizzie told him.

"That's an old wives tale!" laughed Graham.

"It works for me," replied Lizzie, perhaps a little too sharply. Embarrassed, she picked up her little bag of conkers and made her way home.

Lizzie was surprised the next day to see Graham standing on her doorstep.

"Sorry if I offended you," he said. "Just because I don't mind spiders, I should realise that not everyone likes them."

Lizzie shuddered. "I hate even the thought of them."

"I bought you this," said Graham holding out a hand made business card. It had a picture of Spiderman and his phone number. "Keep it handy, just in case the conkers ever let you down."

"Thank you," said Lizzie taking the card. "Actually, I'm glad you've called round because I've got something for you. Come in."

Lizzie led Graham into her little kitchen at the back of the house. "Look!" she said and handed over a mammoth conker.

"Where on earth did you find this?"

"Near the doctor's surgery," Lizzie paused a moment as she looked at her guest. "You can have it, on one condition," she blurted out.

"What's that?" he asked looking up and looking into her eyes. Yes, he did have kind eyes and a gentle face. Since they'd met on Thursday, she'd been unable to get him out of her mind and so she'd done a little research. Retired and widowed just like her, she found out that he lived in a cottage on the outskirts of the village. "On what condition?"

"You use up your windfalls," she told him. "They're just wasted lying around on the grass in your garden."

"I'm not much of a cook. Carole did all that sort of thing."

"Well if you collect them up, I'd be happy to do some baking and split them half and half."

"Deal," said Graham quickly. "I'll go right home and collect them up now."

Graham was as good as his word. He cleared up the apples and delivered them over to Lizzie later that afternoon.

"I'll never eat all that," he told her the following day when he called in to invite her out for a coffee.

Lizzie laughed. "I've done these small ones for you and I to put in the freezer and this large apple pie is for when your family come over from New Zealand."

"Oh, they'll love that," said Graham enthusiastically. "And what's that?"

"I got carried away," admitted Lizzie. "I'd forgotten how much I enjoyed baking and I've made a cake and some biscuits."

"I called in to invite you out for a coffee, but…"

Lizzie smiled and flicked the kettle on. "Have tea and cake with me today and perhaps we could go for a coffee tomorrow?"

"Sounds like a date?" said Graham quietly.

"A date with Spiderman!" mused Lizzie. "I wonder what my grandchildren would say?"

"Is that a problem?" asked Graham anxiously.

"There is one condition," began Lizzie seriously. Graham nodded.

"I had a feeling there might be. Go on."

"You must leave the skin tight Spiderman outfit at home!" Lizzie told him.

"No problem," grinned Graham, with a sigh of relief.

"Then we've got a date,"

With that he punched the air. "I nearly chickened out and didn't say anything, but I know I'd have regretted it if I had."

Graham cut the cake while Liz made the tea. He wore a grin reminiscent of a Cheshire Cat and Lizzie felt a warm glow burning inside her.

First published in *My Weekly 2016 Annual* out in December 2015

Moving Forward

The door-bell chimed and my heart sank. I really didn't feel like seeing anyone. I ignored it, hoping they would go away and leave me alone.

No such luck. Whoever it was, they were persistent. I had a sneaky look out the window. I might have guessed, it was Shona again, from work, looking as glamorous as ever in her uniform. She'd obviously come straight here. I knew she'd stay until I opened the door, so I had no choice.

She didn't bat an eyelid that I was still in my pyjamas at midday, but then we were used to working odd hours.

"Would you like a coffee?" I asked.

"How about I make us both a coffee, while you shower and get dressed?" suggested Shona gently. "I've brought fresh croissants just in case you hadn't had breakfast."

I bit back the tears, nodded and went to have my shower as if I was on automatic pilot, excuse the pun, but Shona and I are air-hostesses.

I could smell the freshly ground coffee as soon as I came downstairs and Shona, bless her, had warmed the croissants and set the table.

We chatted about general things as we shared breakfast. She said everyone was missing me and really sorry about the baby. Sorry! What an empty word. Didn't anyone understand what I was going through?

"I was hoping you'd be ready to come back," began Shona. "It's not the same without you."

"I can't come back," I told her. "I feel as dead as…" I looked around and noticed a bare twig in a pot that Pete had given me for my birthday. "As dead as that plant."

"It might help," she said. "It could take your mind off things."

"I'm not sleeping and that makes me irritable. I'd be no

good dealing with people. I keep snapping at Pete and I know it's not his fault."

"It's no one's fault. It's just one of those awful things, but didn't the doctor say there was no reason why you couldn't carry a healthy baby in future?"

"I still feel so mixed up," I tried to explain. "I feel angry and guilty and so terribly sad. I know it's been a couple of months, but I still can't look at a baby or a pregnant woman and I cry at the silliest of things."

"Will you let me do your hair?" asked Shona, obviously trying to help me change the subject. I shrugged. What did I care?

I think everyone needs a friend like Shona. Every time she had a day off she'd come and visit. At first, I'd been so rude to her but she still came back.

She'd only been with me a couple of hours but she'd got me up and dressed, she soothingly brushed and styled my hair, she insisted I wore a little make-up and then she did my nails.

I couldn't believe it; not only did I look human again but I actually felt hungry. That night I had a better night's sleep, not perfect, but an improvement.

With Shona's support I returned to work. I should have been six months pregnant and glowing but life goes on after miscarriage. I quickly learnt to put on a brave face. Fortunately, I'd done the job for over ten years and knew I could go through the routine even though I was empty inside.

After some time, I was back in my British Airways uniform boarding a 12+ hour flight to Tokyo. Shona was beside me, so I knew I could do it.

We landed after an uneventful flight. I just wanted to sleep but Shona insisted we take the Metro. There was something she wanted to see. I tagged along oblivious to the sights and sounds of Japan.

In less than an hour we were at Hie Shrine. It's such a beautiful place. There were lots of people around but it was quiet and tranquil.

We went through the ritual of hand washing before entering the shrine.

"I'm going to sit here," announced Shona. "Go and find Mizuko Jizo."

A Japanese woman looked up as Shona spoke. The words obviously meant more to her than they did to me. The stranger smiled. She reached out her hand and led me silently to a statue of a monkey wearing a red cape. Beside her was a baby monkey.

"Mizuko Jizo watches over the spirits of dead children" explained the woman before leaving me with the statue.

Funnily enough, it was a great comfort to know there was a word for the child I'd lost – Mizuko. I felt, at last, that someone understood. Not only that, but silly as it may sound, it was important to me to feel that this monkey god was somehow caring for my baby and I could trust her to do that – forever.

You'd think the tears would be a raging tsunami by now, but I felt calm and back in control. I stayed near the Jizo for a while and then I went to find Shona, still sitting where I'd left her.

She smiled and I tried to smile back but it felt odd. I hadn't used those muscles for so long, it ached.

"Home?" she asked.

"Home," I agreed but, on the journey back, it was as though someone had switched on the noise, the colour, and the smells. I was alive again.

I texted Pete as soon as we got to the hotel and sent him a photo Shona had taken of me laughing. I couldn't explain what had happened. I don't think he'd have understood anyway, but that wasn't important any more.

I felt complete and at peace. I would never forget my baby, our baby, but I knew now I had to let go and move on. I knew now I could help Pete with his grieving. We'd be strong and face the "Due Date" together.

Within seconds Pete texted me back not only telling me how much he loved me, but with a picture of the bare twig he'd given me for my birthday and I'd not had the energy to move let alone to water. It was now in flower – an early blossom and a reminder of spring and a fresh start.

First published in *Allas*, Sweden in December 2016

The Secret Everyone Knew

Early 1900s

Molly, the doctor's wife, heard the soft tap on the back door. She picked up the lamp and went to see who was there.

A waif of a girl stood shivering on the kitchen step. She was young, little more than a child. Molly's heart went out to her; the poor girl looked as though she carried the worries of the whole village on her shoulders.

"Come in and warm yourself by the fire," Molly said without a second thought. The girl hesitated. She looked dazzled by the lamplight, and her face was as pale as linen. "You look frozen, come in."

The girl looked behind her; it was dusk, and no one was around. Cautiously she stepped inside the warm kitchen and let herself be led toward the glow of the open fire.

Molly had just made herself a pot of tea; she fetched another cup and poured in the hot dark liquid. It wasn't unusual for patients to call on the doctor at all times, day and night. No matter how tired she felt, she always welcomed them into her home, knowing they may be in great pain.

"Here, drink this, it'll warm your insides."

The girl cradled the cup in her hands, savouring the warmth for some time before she even took a sip.

All the while, Molly was watching her unexpected guest. She was probably not even twenty, and pregnant. In fact, from the swell of her body, her time was nearly up. Her breathing, although a little fast, didn't suggest she was in labour.

"Is it the doctor you've come for?" Molly asked, keeping her voice gentle so as not to frighten the girl.

The girl shook her head. Briefly she raised her eyes to

meet Molly's. There was a pleading look. Molly had seen it many times before. No more needed to be said.

"What can I do for you?" Molly asked. The unfortunate girl looked desperate, her face earnest.

Again, the girl lent forward and looked around, finding the house quiet, she unclenched her fist to reveal a metal ring.

"How much?" she asked in barely a whisper.

Molly took the ring and looked at it more closely by candlelight. It was certainly a pleasing piece of jewellery and unlikely to belong to the waif who sat opposite her. Molly checked herself; she wasn't here to judge. She was here to help. Clearly there was a story here if the girl wished to share her tale.

"How did you come by this?" Molly asked. "Is it stolen?" The girl looked horrified at the thought.

"It's mine, his Lordship said…"

"Do you need food, or money?" Molly asked. She'd noticed the thin gown the girl was wearing, and her lack of shoes. "I can give you a mixture of both, if that would be better?"

The girl seemed indecisive until she glanced at a pie that had recently been removed from the Aga.

Molly nodded just as they were both distracted by the sound of a door opening and closing elsewhere in the building. The doctor had returned.

"Stay here," Molly pushed back her chair and cut a generous slice of the pie, putting it down in front of the lass. "Eat this. I'll just see to the doctor. He's unlikely to come down here. Your secret's safe." Molly smiled and patted the girl's arm. "Don't go away. I'll not be long."

Molly poured another tea and took it to the doctor, who received it gratefully.

"Are you hungry?" she asked him, wondering if she

should mention the lass in the kitchen, but the girl needed practical help, which Molly could administer, not medicine.

"I'm starving, but I've got to go to The Manor; her ladyship's having hysterics. I don't know what's triggered it this time." He gulped down a few sips of tea while he refilled his bag and left a few minutes later.

Molly hurried upstairs to her dressing room, quietly closing the door. Here she had a small bureau which had belonged to her mother and was where she liked to sit and write letters and conduct her household business.

Inside was a hidden compartment. Her mother kept her father's love letters inside, but Molly now used it for secrets of her own.

Rolled up in the little drawer, were several pound notes and a few coins. She took what she needed and hid the rest.

Molly returned to the kitchen. Using her shawl, she filled it with whatever she could spare from her larder.

"Take this," she said handing over the food wrapped in her shawl and the money she'd retrieved from the bureau. "I'll keep the ring for four weeks. If you're not back for it, I'll pass it on to my brother; he's a pedlar. He'll try and get the best price he can. You understand?"

The girl nodded, hugging the shawl full of food. One minute she was there and the next she'd disappeared into the night. Molly wished her God's Speed but wondered if she'd ever see her again.

The following day, Molly polished the ring as best she could. It had a pretty pattern on it and fitted Molly perfectly. Usually, she would place such items in an old tea caddy until her brother was next in town, but before she'd had a chance to do so, there was a loud hammering at the front door.

Slipping the ring on her finger for safe keeping, she

rushed to the door expecting to find a man distraught because his wife had gone into labour or someone with an open wound.

Instead, Constable Perry was just raising his truncheon about to beat once more on her front door.

"Good morning. Can I help?"

"I need the doctor. Is he here?"

Automatically, she surveyed the constable and decided he wanted information rather than treatment, and as such would have to wait his turn.

"He's got a patient," she told him. "He won't be long. Can I get you a cup of tea while you wait?"

"It's of the utmost importance," spluttered the constable. "Her ladyship's been robbed."

Molly hurried away to the kitchen, removing the ring as she did so and placing it in the old tea caddy on the top shelf.

She'd made it her mission to help those in need, just as her husband did, asking no questions and casting no verdict.

For years now, she'd been an unofficial pawnbroker. Any profit she made she ploughed back into helping others. The funds provided for the regular soup kitchen she organised, and it helped restock the chest of children's clothes. Thinking back to the poor girl from the previous night, Molly realised it was time to collect more warm clothes and shoes for distribution to those most needy. Perhaps when her ladyship was feeling better, she would be inclined to donate some cast-offs? It would be the least she could do; she was always calling out the doctor for her minor ailments.

"Here you are," Molly said as she handed the constable a cup of tea, just as Dr Taylor said goodbye to his patient.

They were ensconced in his surgery for a few minutes. At one point, she thought she heard raised voices, but soon after the constable left, practically slamming the door behind him.

Within minutes the constable reappeared at the kitchen door with two of his officers.

"Show me your hands," the constable demanded. Molly did as she was asked, aware of her heart pounding in her chest, making it hard to keep her breathing steady. It took all her might to stop her hands from shaking. To her dismay, she realised the constable must have noticed the ring she'd been wearing.

Her eyes seemed to be drawn to the top shelf. It was all she could do to avoid looking in that direction.

Nevertheless, the officers searched the kitchen from top to bottom. Molly had to stand and watch. She felt helpless. Eventually, they found what they'd been looking for.

"Can you explain how you come to have her ladyship's ring?"

"Her ladyship's ring!" Molly gasped. She thought back to the slip of the girl from the previous night. It was obvious she was with child and presumably had lost her job because of that. Despite her denial, had she stolen the ring? Had the father of her child given it to her, albeit naively, in an effort to help? Or even perhaps as a sign of his feelings for her?

Molly knew she could not allow herself to reveal the visit of the young girl; The girl had troubles enough of her own, poor thing. Molly decided to hold her tongue, putting faith in God and the kindness of human nature.

Doctor Taylor had obviously heard voices and came to see what was going on.

"I'm arresting your wife. She was in possession of her ladyship's ring!" the constable explained triumphantly to the doctor.

"There must be some mistake," began the doctor.

"You'll have to tell that to the judge." The constable nodded to his officers to escort Molly from the premises.

The doctor instantly went for his wallet, but Molly gave him a warning look. He'd also be in trouble if he tried to bribe the constable.

"I haven't done anything wrong," Molly assured him. "Have faith. I'll be back before you know it."

Molly was taken to the police station where she was kept under lock and key. The cell was cold, sparse and dark. She held her head high with what she hoped showed dignity. After all, she knew she hadn't stolen the ring. She'd been nowhere near The Manor in months. No one could prove she'd taken the ring, because she hadn't. She was innocent.

At least this would be a good time to reflect, Molly thought. *There will be few distractions*. She had many things to consider while she sat and waited.

"And what do *you* want?" bellowed the officer to some unsuspecting visitor. Molly couldn't see anyone from her cell, but wondered if someone was coming to her rescue. She had no wish to remain there a moment longer, and was already thinking how she could improve such facilities for others, in the future.

"It's hot broth for Mrs Taylor," a female voice said. "Or *you* could have it, if you set her free." The aroma of rosemary wafted through the air.

"Be off with you!" shouted the officer, but then his voice changed. "Oh, sorry sir."

Molly was heartened to hear her husband's voice, calm and measured as though he were prescribing cough medicine for a child.

"May I speak with my wife?" he asked. "I'll take her this broth. I'm sure she'll be grateful. How kind of the lady to bring it."

"Don't worry Sir, I'll keep it for her, until you're ready

to go," the officer said and Molly's heart sank. She doubted she'd ever get to taste it, nor discover who to thank.

Delighted though she was to see her husband, Molly's thoughts were more about prison reform than her own, temporary incarceration.

"What can I do to set you free?" he asked as he held both her hands, and tenderly kissed her forehead.

"Have you spoken with his Lordship? A *private* word perhaps?" Molly whispered. "He may know something of the ring." If Dr Taylor was surprised, he didn't show it. Instead, he nodded and held her close. There was comfort in his embrace.

"I'll do as you suggest," he said. "I'll go there right away."

Molly didn't sleep much that night. The bench was hard, the blanket thin and there was a constant stream of comings and goings from the police station.

The most frequent visitor was a reporter from the local newspaper. He engaged anyone and everyone in conversation, gleaning fresh gossip all the time. The duty officer refused him access to the prisoner. Not that Molly would have revealed anything, but she might have got him to write a piece about the awful conditions innocent victims were held in, awaiting trial.

Until now, she'd not had time to reflect on the shame attached to being *really* poor. Nor had she considered how her discreet pawn broker services were the secret everyone knew, but no one ever mentioned. People felt humiliated by their circumstances, often through no fault of their own. Molly thought again of the young girl, guessing the father of her child was at the root of this.

There was a change of shift at about midnight. There had been no sign of the warm soup. She dozed, but was too troubled to sleep properly.

Outside a man was calling, "Doctor's wife arrested, read all about it!" During the course of the morning, it was repeated like a mantra. She knew she'd be branded as a common thief despite her standing in society and her unblemished record. She worried how the stigma would affect her husband. How was he coping without her assessing patients as they arrived? Sometimes all they needed was a friendly face to listen to them, and a clean handkerchief to wipe away the tears.

Molly had been confident that somehow her good deeds would be recognised, and she'd be free to return home. But the hours went by.

The court case was looming. It was actually looking more and more likely she would be sent to prison. She asked herself what should she have done differently? She knew she'd been foolish to wear the ring; a moment of vanity. Constable Perry must have seen it, otherwise there would have been no reason to suspect the upstanding doctor's wife.

"And no one can vouch where you were on the evening in question?" the prosecutor asked.

"My husband came home around ten to restock his bag. He's told you I was home. I'd made him a hot pie."

"But no one can verify where you were after his surgery had finished, until he returned at ten, nor your whereabouts between a quarter past ten and midnight when the good doctor returned home to find you asleep in a chair?"

Molly shook her head. She searched the solemn faces opposite her and wondered how long it would be before she was allowed home. Would it really be years?

News travelled fast in the village and before the end of the day there were a line of people queuing up to speak with Constable Perry.

Molly sat on the hard bench in her cell. She could hear every word that was said in the adjacent reception area.

"I found the ring," a woman said with confidence. "I gave it to Mrs Taylor to keep it safe until we found the owner." Molly recognised her voice. It was the milkman's wife. Her husband was a good man, but weak, and liked a drink. More than once he'd spent his weekly wage in the public house without a thought to paying the rent or feeding his family. They would have starved without her help.

Not long afterwards she heard the baker's booming voice, "It fell out of a sack of flour I tell you. A golden ring it was. Mrs Taylor was just looking after it for me, keeping it safe like."

"And where did you get the sack of flour from?" one of the officers asked.

"I have many suppliers," the baker said. "I'm not sure which one had the ring in it. They all look the same to me."

Molly could picture the officer dutifully writing down the baker's statement and getting him to make his mark.

It wasn't long after he'd gone when Matthew the fisherman came in with his two sons. The last time she'd seen Matthew was when he was pawning his boots, so he could put food on the table. Times had been hard of late, the poor man was grieving the loss of his wife, and doing his best for his sons.

"I caught this fish, a whopper it was, and as I went to gut it, a gold ring fell out. My sons saw it too, and we gave it to Mrs Taylor. You can trust her, you can."

Molly felt warmed by the way the villagers were rallying round on her behalf, but hated the thought that any of them would get into trouble for wasting police time or perverting the course of justice.

Dr Taylor visited again. "No joy," he said. "I asked to see His Lordship, but he's away from home. Have you considered…?"

"I can't betray a trust; you of all people must understand?" Molly said, taking her husband's hand.

“Then all we can do is pray,” he said and bowed his head, holding Molly’s hands in his.

Molly woke early the following morning, the day of her sentencing, and wondered what the newspaper seller would be shouting today.

“Abandoned baby! Read all about it.”

Molly’s thoughts returned to the young girl and suspected the child could have been hers. The woman had obviously sacrificed her baby in the hope it would be taken in and given a better life.

The morning dragged. Molly had been perched on the edge of her seat for hours and yet no one had come to escort her to court. The waiting was agony.

By lunchtime, she became aware that something was afoot. Then, to her surprise and delight, an officer came, unlocked the cell and told her she was free to go.

“I don’t understand,” she said as soon as she reached the safety of her home. Dr Taylor took her in his arms. He looked weary and his shirt was creased.

“In the early hours, I delivered a baby boy. The young mother instructed me to take the child to The Manor and present it to his lordship. I must say I was reluctant, but on arriving, the cook said, ‘Not another!’ and the child was taken to a nursery and cared for with his other illegitimate offspring. Officially these are all ‘abandoned’ children”.

“I did wonder,” Molly said sadly. “News travels quickly.”

“I’d also been instructed to deliver a letter to Constable Perry, which I did. The girl explained how His Lordship had given her the ring. She’d mistakenly thought it was a token of love. When she was discarded in favour of another servant, she desperately went to you for help, giving you the ring in return for food, money and warm clothing. Your shawl probably saved her life, and that of the child.”

"And mine too!" laughed Molly. "I'm so relieved to be home." Just as her words were out, they heard a noise coming from downstairs.

"Oh Lord, I forgot, your brother's here," Dr Taylor confessed. "He's been waiting for you in the kitchen."

Molly hurried to meet her brother while Dr Taylor saw to his patients.

"I think it's time," Molly told her brother over a fresh pot of tea. "We need to make things official and open a pawnbroker's shop on the edge of town, and I know of a young woman who's recently lost her job. I think she'd make an ideal assistant for you. It'll be better for us all, if we do this openly from now on. I've had enough of keeping secrets."

The Gentleman Gypsy

1885

"And who is going to look after all your animals while you're away?" The duke listened patiently to his aunt, Lady Somerset. "Even you must realise you cannot take them all in your… what do you call that contraption? Your house on wheels?"

"It's called a caravan. And yes, you're right. I do have a problem. I'll take The Colonel with me, but the others will have to stay. Can't your stable boys take care of them?"

"And who would oversee the stable boys?" Lady Somerset enquired. "They cannot be left to their own devices." The duke nodded. "You do realise there is only one solution, and that's to take a wife."

"It seems rather drastic! I was thinking more of hiring a veterinary doctor, surely that would appear more logical. I mean, what do I want with a wife?"

"The right woman could provide company and entertainment in your latter years," Lady Somerset reached for the cord and rang for Harris to serve tea.

"The *right* woman would accompany me on my travels, and that wouldn't solve our problem of the animals left behind," The duke argued, but he could tell his aunt wasn't convinced, but then she'd been trying to marry him off for years.

"We'll say no more of the matter for now," she told him, "but rest assured I shall come up with the solution. Now, drink your tea."

"I intend to embark on my travels when I hear the first cuckoo." He finished his tea, stood, bowed to his aunt and returned to the cabin he inhabited in the grounds of his home, despite it being the depths of winter.

There was snow on the ground when he was next summoned to take tea with Lady Somerset. Much to his annoyance she was not alone. Opposite her sat the most enormous woman he'd ever set eyes on. She was dressed from head to toe in her black widow's weeds. She reminded him of Queen Victoria.

"Lady Hathaway has seven dogs no less, and many fine thoroughbreds. She was only confiding with me the other day that sometimes she preferred animals to people." Lady Somerset gave a polite laugh.

The duke, however, had already come to the conclusion that animals were often preferable to humans. He gazed out of the window. From his vantage point he could just see the chimneys of his own property.

Some years previously the duke had built a small dwelling in his grounds. The little wooden cabin was where he spent most of his time and where he felt happiest during the winter months when the English climate forced him to remain at home. It had a decent fireplace, a good mattress and a pulley system of bells rigged up to the main house in case he needed a servant.

To his surprise when he eventually turned around to ask Harris to refill his tea cup, he realised he had been left alone with Queen Victoria. He knew he was required to make polite conversation. All he could hope was that Lady Somerset would soon return and rescue him from this impossible situation.

The duke listened politely as Lady Hathaway described each of her dogs in great detail. It took all his willpower not to yawn. He briefly wondered what his own dog, The Colonel, would think of her, but as they were never likely to meet, it was a pointless exercise.

The thought of having Lady Hathaway as his companion filled him with dread; her voice was monotonous and she had hairs on her chin! Besides, his Minha bird would easily be able to mimic her, and that would cause no end of trouble. The match was doomed.

"I take it she was not to your liking." The duke could feel his aunt's eyes on him and knew she wasn't happy. "Fortunately for you I have met the perfect match."

The duke sighed but knew his aunt well enough to know there was no point arguing and as yet he had not found anyone suitable to look after his growing menagerie of animals until his return in late autumn.

The second candidate he was introduced to was even more unsuitable than the first. She resembled a fragile sparrow, and looked as eager to fly away.

One glance at her and he could tell she would take an instant dislike to The Colonel, the duke's faithful friend, a bulldog. He also knew that if he were ever in a situation, God forbid, that he would have to choose between The Colonel and this birdlike creature, then Heaven help him but he would choose his dog.

Furthermore, the woman was unlikely to be able to round up a donkey; and the goats would run rings around her. In fact, they would positively enjoy stealing her bonnet to nibble at, or giving her a nudge as she refilled their water trough. No, in his opinion, she wasn't up to the job of caring for his animals.

"I appreciate your help in this matter, but have no fear, for today I have instructed The Times newspaper to run a suitable advertisement for an animal lover to reside at The Wilderness from spring to autumn each year. I am confident I shall find the perfect gentleman."

"And where will they live during the winter?" Lady Somerset asked.

The duke shrugged. "That is not my problem. I merely require part-time help."

"But a house needs to be managed all year round whether you are living there or not," Lady Somerset informed him. "And even a jungle needs a little attention from a gardener now and again."

The duke stood up tall. It was all he could do to remain civil to his aunt. He knew she had his best intentions at heart, but he felt she clearly did not understand he did not want her gardeners tidying up his land while he was away.

He finished his tea and shortbread, and took his leave at the earliest opportunity.

On arriving back home to the aptly named "Wilderness" all he wanted was to hide away in the cabin at the end of the garden. His easel was set up and he felt inspired to continue working on his portrait of The Colonel asleep by the fireside.

Much to his dismay he could hear voices as he approached his gate. Furthermore, it appeared John, his coachman and Foley, his valet were engaged in conversation with a woman. He could definitely hear a lady's voice and he had had more than his fair share of female company to last him a lifetime, and that was all down to his aunt and her meddlesome ways.

The duke, unlike his uncle, was not portly, but trim. He was a tall man and it was his height that gave him away as he tried to discreetly avoid the main house and make for his bolthole. He'd hoped the overgrown bushes would hide him from his servants and whoever was with them.

"I am just on my way, sir," the woman said with a nod. The duke thought she looked vaguely familiar. He was pleased to see she was neither the replica of Queen Victoria nor the size of a sparrow. "I had no wish to disturb you. Good day."

"Miss Partridge has very kindly brought you her late father's fishing rod," his coachman explained.

"I felt it would be of more use to you on your travels, than to me." She gave a little smile and he realised where he'd set eyes on this maiden before. She was, of course, the late vicar's daughter.

"You won't be taking after your father and fishing for carp in the lakes?" he teased.

"I prefer my fish alive and swimming. Good day to you, Your Grace." With that she turned and within seconds was hidden from view in the undergrowth of his overgrown garden. The duke watched as a small spaniel obediently trotted along after her just as The Colonel followed him.

The duke could not understand it, but he was plagued by the image of that woman. She pervaded his dreams at night and by day his subconscious sought her out in the market place. There was something enchanting about the woman; even her name pleased him, Miss Partridge.

"John," he said a few days later as together they were beginning to furnish the ornate, but practical, caravan ready for their travels. "Tell me all you know of Miss Partridge."

"Being the vicar's only daughter, she is next to godliness itself. She is tireless in helping others. Only last night she sat at the bedside of Mrs Chapple as she gave birth to another strapping son. Then, while Mrs Chapple slept it was Miss Partridge herself who prepared a meal for Mr Chapple and fetched the church charity box of baby clothes for his new son."

"I seem to recall she's no stranger in a saddle."

"She rides a mare like there's no tomorrow, but all that will change when she leaves for the north."

"She's leaving?"

"A new family are due at the vicarage by Lady Day. There was some talk of her becoming a governess but…"

"She's an animal lover?"

"Without doubt," John admitted. "She impressed me by naming all the birds in the mulberry tree. The only other person I can recall who can do that is Your Grace, sir."

"I should like you to take an invitation to Miss Partridge. I wish to give her a tour of the garden and to take tea with me in the cabin." The duke waved his arms like a magician and was surprised to see the hesitation in his coachman. "What's the matter man? Is she betrothed to another?"

"I'll send a message forthwith," John replied.

"Hold on a moment! Is it customary for me to give her a gift?"

"I don't believe it necessary when one's invited her to tea but…"

"Yes?"

"I do believe Miss Partridge sketches, and she has made enquiries in the past about drawing Delilah the donkey. Perhaps you could grant her permission?"

"Was she the woman, some time ago, who requested Delilah went to church on Palm Sunday?"

"That is correct, your Grace. You declined the offer telling her Delilah, as far as you knew, was atheist."

"Did I indeed? I don't suppose that went down very well."

"On the contrary, your Grace, she found it most amusing."

"What are you hanging around for man? Give her my invitation and tell her to bring her sketch book and that little dog of hers."

The duke and Miss Partridge got on famously, both sharing a love of animals and the arts. Henceforth Miss Partridge took to visiting each afternoon to take tea.

One day they were strolling round the garden admiring the snowdrops when they were interrupted by a dreadful scream.

"Whatever is that?" Miss Partridge enquired. "Have you bought yourself a peacock?" He shook his head as they heard another wail coming from the boundary with Lady Somerset's property. The duke looked at Miss Partridge to see if she was distressed by the outcry, but rather than fainting at the sound, she went in search of the source.

A muntjac deer was ensnared in a tangle of brambles and stinging nettles.

"May I borrow your coat?" Miss Partridge asked. Without a second thought the duke removed his coat and handed it over. Miss Partridge draped it over the frightened animal's head which instantly produced a calming effect. She knelt and spoke quietly to the creature, gently stroking and reassuring him with one hand while she plucked at some dock leaves with the other.

Emmeline Partridge rubbed the deer with the cooling dock leaf until he relaxed. Together they eased the poor creature out of the brambles. Then the duke's coat slipped and the deer bolted like a bullet from a poacher's gun and he ran off into the wilderness.

The duke retrieved his coat, dusted it off and put it back on.

"Our good deed for the day I think," he said. "And now it's time for tea. I've asked for gingerbread as you said you were partial to it."

"How very kind and thoughtful of you,"

"One good deed, deserves another," the duke said and offered Miss Partridge his arm.

By the end of the second week, he did something preposterous, and proposed.

"I am in such a quandary," Emmeline Partridge admitted. "For I have grown rather fond of you Sir, and look forward to each afternoon spent with you…"

"So, what could possibly be the problem?"

"My father brought me up to serve the community which I do with a glad heart. If I were to marry you, I expect you'd want me to accompany you on your travels and being your wife, I would have to agree, but I feel my duty lies in serving the poor and needy."

"And what if I travelled alone, leaving you for half the year as housekeeper in charge of my animals and servants? You could then continue with your charitable works and I would have the pleasure of your company from Michaelmas to Easter?"

"That would seem an ideal situation, would it not?" Emmeline replied.

"And would you write to me?"

"Daily," Miss Partridge promised. "I might even illustrate my letters."

The duke glanced over at the fireplace where The Colonel was curled up beside Simeon the spaniel.

"In that case, will you accompany me to call on my aunt, Lady Somerset? I should like her to give us her blessing, and I can introduce you to her donkey, Samson, who would probably welcome being in a Nativity as well as attending St. Mary's on Palm Sunday."

The Pram Race

June 1953

"I'm not doing it!" George said. "And that's final."

"But we'll be the only ones not taking part," Rita told him. "It'll be disrespectful to the new Queen!"

"What a load of rubbish," he scoffed. "If you want to do it, I won't stop you, but count me out."

Rita was close to tears, she'd been so looking forward to having some fun on Coronation Day and when the vicar's wife came up with this idea, she'd been really excited.

It wouldn't be the same without George. She could ask Mr Wilson, the butcher. He'd been a widower for years, brought up his sons more or less on his own and yet always maintained his cheery manner. Would it cause too much gossip if she approached him?

Rita left it a day or two hoping George's friends and his brother would help change his mind. She should have known; George could be so stubborn at times.

"Good afternoon, Rita," Mr Wilson greeted her with a warm smile. It made her feel good, although she was well aware he was the same with everyone. "What can I do for you? Nice sausages for George?"

"Actually, it's a favour I wanted to ask," she began. "You know Mrs Robinson's organised a pram race on Coronation Day?"

Mr Wilson shook his head. Rita felt herself blush, of course no one would have mentioned it to him because it was for couples.

"Well, the idea is for men to dress up as a nanny and push their wives, dressed as babies, around the village, in a pram. They're to stop at each pub along the way and down a half pint before moving on. The winning pair become King and Queen for the street party and get to sit at the top table."

"I see," he said slowly, but Rita could tell he hadn't really understood her dilemma.

"George refuses point blank to dress up," she blurted out. "He said he wouldn't stand in my way, if I wanted to take part."

"And you're asking me to take George's place, dress like a woman and push you from pub to pub drinking ale as quickly as I can?"

"That's about it." Rita gave him a little smile. When he put it like that, it did sound ridiculous.

"I'd like to help you out," he began, "but I don't drink. I haven't let a drop touch my lips since I lost my Lizzie and I don't intend to start now."

"Of course," Rita said. "I shouldn't have asked. I'm sorry."

Now she felt truly awful, as she remembered he'd been out drinking when his wife died, not that anyone knew she had a bad heart and would drop down dead that particular evening.

"I tell you what though," Mr Wilson smiled and his eyes twinkled. "Maybe if you tell George, you've asked me and that it really warmed my heart to feel wanted, perhaps he'd change his mind?"

"Oh Mr Wilson, that's a splendid idea!" Rita beamed at him. "I'll give it a try."

"I thought I looked stupid." George laughed as he looked down at his white gloves and brown dress with a crisp white apron. "But Reverend Robinson looks a real sight!"

"I actually thought it was his mother!" Rita admitted. "I only just managed to stop myself from greeting her."

"I thought you were meant to be dressed as a baby," George said as he looked more closely at Rita.

"I opted to wear red, white and blue instead," she said as she straightened her red crepe paper hat. She'd bought it in Woolworth's, and was delighted to get the last one.

George gallantly helped Rita into their old pram. Their children were ten and twelve now and it had been gathering cobwebs.

"It's come up a real treat," he said proudly as he carefully pushed her to the start line.

Bunting flapped in the breeze and families lined the streets waving their flags. Everyone had been up early polishing their doorsteps, baking cakes and generally preparing for the day of festivities.

The pram race had to be early in order to be finished in time for those who wanted to watch the main part of the coronation on the television.

The coronation and how the village would celebrate it, had been the main, if not the only, topic of conversation for many months. And, just when everything seemed to be sorted, a group of church ladies questioned the fact that the public houses should not be serving so many pints to so many men so early in the day.

The church ladies pointed out that the consumption of alcohol might well make the men ill, and it was certainly not setting a good example to the youth in the village, nor being respectful to their new Queen.

Despite the majority of the inhabitants being willing to turn a blind eye to all this, because it was such a mementos occasion, it was the church ladies who were victorious.

They approached the vicar's wife who had come up with the idea of the pram race in the first place. Mrs Robinson tried to negotiate a compromise, but the church ladies were adamant, and Mrs Robinson couldn't argue with their objections.

Reluctantly, she had agreed that the men should be served water instead, although she suspected not all publicans would adhere to this last-minute change of plans, not that any of the participants would object.

Rita smiled when she heard the outcome; if it had been water from the start, Mr Wilson would probably have been the one pushing the pram instead of George, but nothing needed to be said. As soon as sweet rationing ended in February, Rita had been sure to slip Mr Wilson's children the occasional sixpence when no one was looking; those boys were a real credit to him.

Mr Wilson rang the school bell to start the race; first stop was The Royal Oak where George downed his first half pint in record time. They were one of the first to head off for The Shoulder of Mutton at the bottom of the hill.

It was then it started to rain, just a few drops, but there were ominous black clouds in the distance.

They were still up with the leaders when they reached The Crown and the rain began to get heavier. But, once George had agreed to participate, he did so to win. He was in and out of the pub within seconds and they made their way to The Dog. The pavements were slippery and the cobbled street at the bottom didn't help, but Rita held on tight.

She only let go when George ran inside for his next half. It was then she noticed red streaks on her white blouse and over one arm. For a moment she thought it was blood, but then to her horror, she realised the red dye in the crepe paper hat had run and stained her top. It would be a devil of a job to get out!

There was no time to do anything but hold tight as George grabbed the pram and headed toward The Mermaid, taking the corner a little too sharply. If it hadn't been for Tony the milkman coming up on the inside, she'd have toppled out, instead the prams scraped each other but remained stable.

They reached the final pub, neck and neck with Tony, and Arthur from the hardware shop. They were seasoned drinkers and their drink didn't touch the sides. George managed to overtake Arthur but Tony just beat him to the finish line.

"I'm sorry love," George said to Rita. "I know you wanted to be Queen of the street party."

Rita lent to kiss his cheek but he held her back. "What's all that red?"

"Don't panic," she said, although his face had gone as white as the froth on a pint. He'd never liked the sight of blood. "It's only where the colour's run. I hope I can get the stain out."

He lent forward and hugged her. He wasn't good with words, but she knew he'd been concerned.

"Come on, let's get you home," he told her, and gently nudged her in the right direction. "I think you need to go and look at yourself in the mirror! I guess you'll want to change before you frighten the children!"

A little later, looking a bit pink in the face, Rita came down the stairs in the dress she'd made especially for the occasion using scraps of red, white and blue material. She was pleased with the way it had turned out, and hoped it would detract people from looking at her dye-stained face.

"That's better," George told her. "And guess what? I've managed to get you a consolation prize."

"What are you talking about?" Rita laughed, but was relieved to hear George hadn't taken the pram race result too seriously.

"We might not be seated at the head of the table for the street party, but I have managed to get you the best seat in the house – right in front of the television at number seven."

Mr and Mrs Harris at number seven were the only people they knew with a television. It had been bought especially for the Coronation, and was a 12" black and white model, in a smart wooden cabinet. The Harrises were childless, and decided to treat themselves now they were getting older. They generously opened their little home up to any of their neighbours who wanted to come and see the Queen being crowned. For many, it was the first time they'd actually seen a television, let alone watched a programme!

The rain hadn't eased off. While the pram race had been going on, those not involved, had been moving the tables and chairs from the High Street into the Scout Hut for an impromptu indoor tea.

"Go on and make yourself comfy," George told her. "Mrs Harris is expecting you; I'll fetch you a plate of food and check up on Peter and Jane." The children had been watching the pram race with their aunt and cousins.

Mrs Harris, who had always had a soft spot for George, because he helped her with her groceries. He always made sure he carried the heavy sack of potatoes after Mr Harris had dug them up from the allotment.

Rita gently tapped on the open door of number seven. "Mrs Harris? May I come in?"

"Of course," Mrs Harris greeted her. "Your George has been in to see me. Follow me." She led Rita into their front sitting room and insisted Rita sat in the centre of the settee right in front of the small screen which was in the process of warming up.

"We'd have had it on at 5.30 am this morning if I'd let her," laughed Mr Harris. "I told her she could listen to the wireless instead. After all it was only 'music while you wait' on the television at that hour."

"Make yourself comfy love," Mrs Harris said as the room began to fill up with neighbours each carrying plates of food over from the Scout Hut.

Rita looked around. She was enjoying the happy atmosphere. It was so good to celebrate this historic day with their family, friends and neighbours.

She spotted Mr Wilson in the doorway and moved up so he could sit beside her. It was the least she could do; he'd certainly played his part in making the day special for her.

Rita's children, Peter and Jane came and sat down on the floor near her feet. They too had plates of food, even though it was still early in the day.

George came in a few moments later, his rain coat dripping wet but with a dry plate of food fit for his queen!

"Oh George, you're my hero!" Rita told him just as the music started, and the commentator announced they were about to witness Princess Elizabeth as she entered Westminster Abbey to be crowned, Queen Elizabeth ll.

Moving On

"Any luck?" Ian asked Jennie. She shook her head.

"He didn't sound very interested, but to be fair I could hear the twins giggling in the background."

"Well, whatever they were doing would be more exciting to James than sorting out his belongings."

"I told him he could look through the boxes when they come over for lunch on Sunday."

Jennie always looked forward to seeing her son and grandchildren. She still wasn't quite sure about Louise, her daughter-in-law. The truth was, Jennie had been fond of the previous long-term girlfriend and had never really come to terms with the fact she'd gone off with James' best friend.

Ian and Jennie spent the week sorting out the spare room and the garden shed.

They'd lived in their current house for thirty years. It had four bedrooms and a large garden which had been great while James was growing up, but he left home over ten years ago and now had a family of his own.

"I want to spring clean the whole house before we invite the estate agent round and I can't do that until James has been through his room."

"If he hasn't collected his stuff in all this time," Ian told her, "then I'd chuck the lot."

"I can't get rid of his guitar and…"

"He's played that instrument once, and that was just to impress his girlfriend. We could put an advert in the convenience store window or take it to the charity shop."

Jennie wasn't so sure she should get rid of his belongings without his permission. She knew she'd feel awful if she'd donated his old toys to some worthy cause and then he'd decided he wanted them for his own children.

"It's not as if we haven't given him tons of opportunities to clear his room, but he's never shown the slightest interest," Ian reminded her and Jennie had to agree.

The following morning, she was up early and, in the mood, to get on with the job. She started with his wardrobe and soon filled two sacks with old clothes.

Meanwhile Ian collected up all his school files, university papers and a bag of miscellaneous wires and broken Air-fix models.

By lunchtime it was satisfying to see how much larger the room looked now it had been decluttered and aired. There were still boxes for him to go through, but they'd made a great start.

"I wish we'd done this years ago," Jennie confessed. Ian nodded but they both knew there were several more boxes up in the attic with his name on.

Somehow, on Sunday, James never managed to get up in the loft, but Louise offered to drop a box of China ornaments off at the charity shop the following day.

The next few months seemed to disappear. Jennie and Ian cleared the house enough for the estate agent to estimate its value. In due course they put it on the market and began the search for a new home.

There were a couple of false starts along the way with couples making offers and then changing their minds. Finally, a family from round the corner offered a good price and, at long last, things began to get moving.

Around this time two things happened. Jennie noticed a local builder putting the finishing touches to a cul-du-sac of ten new houses.

The other occurrence was a visit from daughter-in-law, Louise. She stood on their doorstep looking sheepish.

"Oh no," thought Jennie. What's she been up to? Her

thoughts flashed back to James' previous love and how she'd broken his heart.

"Ages ago you gave me a box to take to the charity shop," Louise began. Jennie had forgotten all about the incident, after all she'd donated her unwanted China ornaments and never expected to hear or see any of them again.

"I put the box in the garage and forgot about it," Louise confessed. "Then, when I came across it last week, I had a better look, and thought you'd do better to sell them online."

"I wasn't looking to make money," Jennie told her. "I just wanted to be able to dust my window sills."

"I know I should just have done as you asked, but here you are," with that Louise held up a fist full of ten-pound notes.

"Wow! I don't know what to say," Jennie said as she invited her daughter-in-law inside. "Why don't we split it between the twins and put it in their savings accounts?"

"That's very kind. Thank you," Louise said as she awkwardly gave Jennie a hug.

"It's turning out to be quite a day," Jennie told her over a coffee. "The solicitor's just called to say we're due to exchange on Friday and move next week."

"That's great news," Louise agreed and they swapped their coffee cups for glasses of champagne.

However, the following week the builder announced a delay… an unforeseeable problem.

"We'll see what we can do," he said. "But realistically we're looking at between two and six weeks before you can move in."

"But that's no good," Jennie told him. "We're moving out of our house on Friday and if we were to rent somewhere they want us to sign up for a minimum of six months."

"All right," the foreman told them, "I'll get my best men and we'll aim for completion in two weeks, but I can't make a promise."

Jennie and Ian thanked him and crossed their fingers. It was time to pay James a visit.

"In theory it should only be for a week," Jennie told him. "We complete on our house on Friday and hopefully the new one will be ready the following week. If we could just store our things in your garage and shed and stay with you for about..."

"Of course, you can," said Louise while James stood with an open mouth. "It'll be lovely to have you." Jennie gave her a hug and realised it was easier this time.

Ian chose to spend most of the week at the allotment but Jennie was determined to help her daughter-in-law with the grandchildren.

"As soon as they've outgrown something I sell it online," Louise told her mother-in-law. "I've got into good habits since I sold your old ornaments. I realised how simple it was."

"You'll be pleased you did so; when they're old enough to leave home they won't leave so much behind."

Jennie thoroughly enjoyed her week with her grandchildren. It was a bonus to really get to know Louise too, but things turned a bit sour when they eventually got hold of the builder and he admitted they'd be at least another month, if not six weeks before the new house was ready.

As much as Louise had made them feel welcome, Jennie did notice how pale she'd gone at the thought of hosting her in-laws for so long. Their home wasn't really big enough for four adults and two small children.

"No problem," Ian said quickly. "We'll go away on a cruise. Then we'll be out of your way."

Four weeks later Ian and Jennie arrived refreshed from their holiday, with a hired van. They loaded up their belongings.

"Give us a long weekend to unpack and get straight, then bring the twins round to play in the garden. It's not huge, but I know just the place for a swing," said Ian with a wave. Jennie hugged Louise warmly.

"Thank you so much for having us, and all our things," Jennie said as she joined Ian in the van.

"Hey Dad!" called James just as Ian was about to pull away.

"There are loads of boxes still in the garage."

"Yes son," Ian said, without switching off the engine, "they're yours. Bye."

Ten out of Ten

Gillian watched as Mr Hammond, the chief accountant, shook Paul's hand. They'd been ensconced in his office for at least half an hour.

Mr Hammond spoke with his secretary and before long she'd typed up a memo for the staff notice board; Paul had been given a special assignment starting 1st January 1971.

Gillian wished Mr Hammond had noticed how she was always first to arrive in the mornings, and last to leave at night. Or how her end of month ledgers always balanced, and that her figures were neatly written, so you could clearly see the pounds, shillings and pence columns.

"Congratulations," Gillian said to Paul with a deep sigh. "That'll stand you in good stead for promotion."

"I hope so," Paul grinned, "although, I feel a bit out of my depth."

During the last days of 1970 between Christmas and New Year, the office was returned to its usual orderly space after the annual Christmas Party.

"I missed you at the party," Paul said as he and Gillian moved a table back into position.

"I had to leave early," Gillian whispered, "to catch the bus. My mother would never have forgiven me if I'd not made it home for Christmas."

"It was a shame, because I hoped we'd have a dance."

Gillian looked up at him. She'd always thought him good looking, with his dark, wavy hair, although rather too serious. No doubt he'd think himself above the office clerks now that he was to get his own office.

"Are we moving your desk somewhere?" Gillian asked, ignoring his talk of dancing.

"This new role is to train up a group of ladies to become

'Decimal Pennies'. I'll be based in the Personnel Department."

"Pardon?" Gillian was well aware of decimalisation taking place in mid-February. It had caused them hours of extra work preparing the accounts department for the changeover.

"Not everyone, it seems, will pick it up as quickly as we do. In order to help our customers, we are to provide a team of suitably qualified young ladies to float around the store offering help if anyone appears confused by the new prices."

"But I thought the idea was to have posters and conversion tables on display everywhere, even in the staff canteen." Gillian pointed to one such poster on the wall.

"All I'm doing is training up these new girls, so they're really confident with the new coins, and their values."

"Well, good luck with that." She laughed. "My Mum's in a real tizz, and my Pa thinks shopkeepers will use it as an excuse to increase prices."

The accounts department didn't seem quite the same to Gillian without Paul sitting at his desk. Mr Hammond said he'd given the job to Paul because he was their brightest mathematician. There was no denying he was clever. He frequently added and subtracted in his head rather than using the adding machine.

At the end of the day Gillian hurried for the bus and was surprised to find Paul in the queue behind her.

"You don't usually catch this one," she said as she made room for him to sit next to her. He looked confused, but then grinned.

"That tops it all," he said with a smile. "I've had the most awful day, and now I've caught the wrong bus."

"It stops round the corner; you can get off there."

"Can I persuade you to come for a drink? I'm in dire need of cheering up."

"I'd love a Baby-cham!" Gillian smiled.

"I had a group of eight young ladies in the boardroom. I went through all the coins and we did a bit of role play, just like the training we all had. I thought it was going to be easy."

"But?"

"Well, they just don't get it. They can't seem to understand you need to forget about counting in twelves and think in tens."

"I suppose it's simple for us, because we're used to dealing with numbers," Gillian admitted. "I know it's not that straight-forward. My mum was muddling everything up thinking there were twenty pennies in a pound instead of 100."

"I don't know what I'm going to do tomorrow; they're meant to be on the shopfloor ready to help. I've asked them all to come in an hour early, but I'm not sure how to make them understand."

The following morning Gillian waited for Paul at the staff entrance.

"I telephoned my mum last night and asked how she was getting on with the new money." Paul looked quite worried. "Don't worry, she told me what's really helped her. I'll ask Mr Hammond if I can help you."

Gillian entered the boardroom and wheeled a record player in on a trolley. Eight glamorous women turned to look in her direction.

"Good morning, ladies," she said as she plugged in the record player, and took a record out of its sleeve. "I'm sure you've all heard Max Bygraves' decimalisation song on the radio?"

They nodded; it had been playing for months.

Carefully she moved the arm of the stereo and gently put the needle down to play the catchy song. As they listened, she untied a roll of wallpaper to reveal the lyrics…

Fortunately, the girls already knew the song, so Gillian pointed out the lines they needed to remember: *There's a hundred new pennies now for every pound.* And then *Five new pence is like a shilling...*

"So, ten bob is now fifty new pence?" one girl said. "I see it now. It's not so hard."

Rather later than planned, a group of pretty shop assistants in straw hats, could be seen dancing their way down the stairs and into the various departments singing *The Decimalisation Song.*

Paul spent the morning wandering around the store, but by lunchtime he'd returned to his desk.

"That was quick work," Mr Hammond said. "I hear our Decimal Pennies have gone down very well." Once again, the chief accountant held out his hand to Paul.

"Actually, I can't take the credit," he was quick to say.

"No. I understand you owe a lot to Max Bygraves," Mr Hammond chuckled.

"I do, but just as much to Gillian. She's not only good with numbers, but excellent with people. She knew exactly how to get the message across."

Mr Hammond looked awkward, but after a deep breath, he turned to face Gillian, as if noticing her for the first time, and held out his hand.

"I can see Paul might not be the only person to consider for promotion, if a vacancy arises."

That evening Gillian skipped down the stairs to catch the bus. Paul was waiting.

"What's your excuse for catching the wrong bus tonight?" she asked with a twinkle in her eye.

"The least I can do is invite you to dinner. Friday night at the Berni Inn?"

"You do realise we're competitors?" she warned him.

"I certainly do, and may the best… person win," Paul said. "But in the meantime, I'd like to thank you for your help today."

"I've still got that Decimalisation song going round in my head!" Gillian admitted.

"Me too," laughed Paul. It was the first time she'd seen him laugh; he usually looked so stern.

"Ride to the first stop with me, and this time I'll buy you a drink. We can decide what to eat on Friday," Gillian suggested.

"I can't think why Mr Hammond thought you'd be too shy to be office manager," he laughed.

"He considered *me* for office manager?"

"He's *still* considering you." Paul paused briefly before adding, "I think you'll set us all a good example. I know I'd give you ten out of ten."

About the Author

As a child Sarah Swatridge had an imaginary friend called Charlie who lived under the bath with his family. Ever since then, she's been creating unusual characters and setting them in awkward situations, challenging them to come through it all with a smile on their face.

Her librarian parents encouraged her. She grew up in a house full of books and her mother, Betty O'Rourke, was also a published writer. They bought her an electric typewriter for her 21st and she's never looked back.

Sarah now has ten Large Print novels on the library shelves published by Ulverscroft. She's had more than a hundred short stories published in women's magazines, worldwide, and a number of plays performed by theatrical groups.

Having studied history at Reading University, she's often drawn back to the past for her inspiration. She now lives in a quiet village with her sports-mad husband and feels blessed to have both her sons and their lovely long-term girlfriends within walking distance.

If you've enjoyed Sarah Swatridge's style, you'll find longer stories (novellas) in the Large Print section of your local library.

You'll find more short stories from Sarah on the Café Lit Magazine website http://cafelit.co.uk.

Her novels are available on Amazon bookstore.

Like to Read More Work Like This?

Then sign up to our mailing list and download our free collection of short stories, *Magnetism*. Sign up now to receive this free e-book and also to find out about all of our new publications and offers.

Sign up here:
http://eepurl.com/gbpdVz

Please Leave a Review

Reviews are so important to writers. Please take the time to review this book. A couple of lines is fine.

Reviews help the book to become more visible to buyers. Retailers will promote books with multiple reviews.

This in turn helps us to sell more books… And then we can afford to publish more books like this one.

Leaving a review is very easy.

Go to https://amzn.to/3SRGBCQ, scroll down the left-hand side of the Amazon page and click on the 'Write a customer review' button.

Other Publications by Bridge House Imprints

The Story Weaver

by Sally Zigmond

Story-telling has often been associated with weaving and spinning. All is craft, cleverness and magic.

Here indeed we have a colourful mix of beautifully crafted stories. Some are sad and others bring us hope. There are tensions in relationships, fear of the unknown coupled with surprising empathy, and accidents of birth. Death wishes are reversed, sometimes but not always, and so are lives in other realties. People's stories intersect as they wait for a bus. An old cello causes havoc. A church clock always strikes twice… or does it? Match-making goes wrong until it goes right. And so much more.

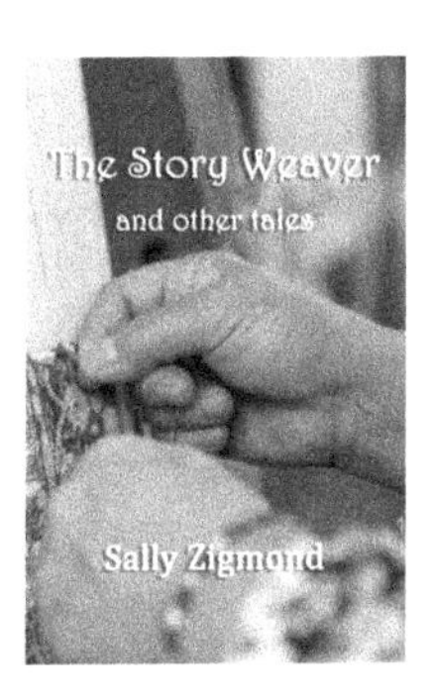

"A wonderful collection of interesting tales. A real mixture that will delight all readers." *(Amazon)*

Order from Amazon:

Paperback: ISBN 978-1-914199-54-7
eBook: ISBN 978-1-914199-55-4

Seen Through a Glass of Red

by Liz Cox

Prepare to suspend your disbelief, have the tissues handy and allow your imagination to run wild. This mix of stories will delight you, make you laugh, make you cry and make you cry out – not really!

From a woman who finds a giraffe under the canal bridge and two cats squabbling over a pancake, to an arrogant French chef and a pair of abandoned sparkly trainers, this collection will make you laugh out loud and touch your heart. You will feel intrigued by a French ghost, visit medieval Denmark at Yul, and the war-torn Middle East. You will even find romance with a green-eyed angel. These are just some of the stories you can expect to find in this collection.

"Thoroughly enjoyed all the stories. Only took me a few hours to read as I couldn't put it down." (*Amazon*)

Order from Amazon:

Paperback: ISBN 978-1-915762-07-8
eBook: ISBN 978-1-915762-08-5

Chapeltown Books

Old Man Jasperson

by Jim Bates

In this collection, Jim looks into what it means to be human in this day and age. How do we cope with the loss of a loved one? What brings us joy? How important is friendship? Can Nature heal?

These are heavy questions, and Jim tackles them head-on with stories that are both intriguing and entertaining. He is not afraid to delve deep into life's challenges. He looks at love and loss, our hopes and dreams, and our own inner fears. Ultimately, his stories show us the strength of the human character.

These stories are heartfelt, and told with quiet passion and a gentle touch. In the end, they resonate with Jim's appreciation for the challenges we all face and, ultimately, the beauty of what it means to be truly alive and to live in this world.

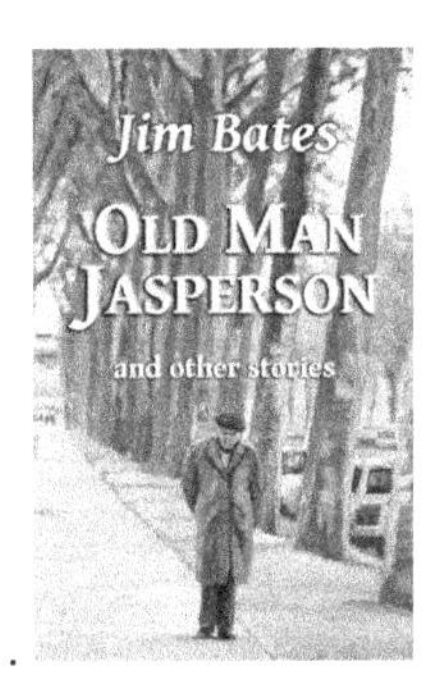

Order from Amazon:

Paperback: ISBN 978-1-914199-46-2
eBook: ISBN 978-1-914199-47-9

Milton Keynes UK
Ingram Content Group UK Ltd.
UKHW020933040924
447871UK00011B/200